THE AWAKENING &
THE SHIP WITH BLACK SAILS

Available now! Don't miss Black OPS by Sammie D!

Visit https://www.comsparc.com/sammied for more details

THE AWAKENING

Chapter One

Rolf awoke at dusk and made his way down the long staircase to his kitchen. Pressing a lever at the bottom of the ice box, a hidden drawer containing several plastic containers of blood revealed itself. After he quenched his thirst, he sat down at his desk to reflect on his dreams from the night before. Visions of a woman with long blonde hair and sad blue eyes haunted him. He didn't know why he continued to have these dreams. He had no idea who this woman was. He had never seen her before; he was sure of that.

Rolf's thoughts went back to his blood supply. He would need to replenish soon. It had been fifty years since he'd fed on living victims. After seven hundred years, he had decided to go against his nature and not kill in order to feed. Several of his brothers and sisters had turned against him—accused him of being soft. *I'm not soft*...he scowled to himself. He was just fascinated by humans, especially by the woman in his dreams.

A soft knock at the door brought Rolf back to the moment. He'd been expecting Kyle, one of the few humans who wasn't afraid of the dark side. Kyle was a scientist, a chemist. They were working together for a cure to Rolf's sensitivity to light.

"What's going on Rolf? You seem a million miles away," Kyle asked as he sat across from his friend.

"Sorry old boy. Just thinking…"

"You've had the dream again, haven't you?"

"Yes. They get more vivid each time."

"And you're sure she's not someone from your past? Surely, you can't remember everyone you've met in the eight hundred plus years you've been a vampire. Or, maybe she's someone from your mortal life."

"I do remember, yet I'm sure I've never seen her before. She has to be important somehow. I guess I just have to wait." Rolf stared off into nothingness for a moment. "How is the serum coming along?"

"I think we should be able to try a run in the sun in about two days."

"Wonderful, I think if this works, maybe I'll end up getting some answers to my dreams."

"I hope so brother."

"I'm going to head down to the club later."

"Rolf, I think the club was a great idea."

"It's too early to tell. Some of my brothers and sisters still like the hunt and kill."

"Do you miss it?"

"Sometimes I do, when I see one of the others enjoying their prey," Rolf admitted.

Chapter Two

Rolf arrived at the Vamp Den around 10:30 that evening. The bar was packed with both humans and vampires. Some of the mortals actually believed that they were creatures of the night. They weren't served the special blends—just Bloody Marys. Mortals wanting to be something they weren't amused Rolf, especially since they had no idea what immortality entailed. He mused over his desire to return to mortality, he longed for a normal life.

William, Rolf's office manager, joined him in his office with a glass and a bottle of Rolf's brand. As he served him he filled Rolf in on the events of the day, "All in all, it has been pretty quiet. They delivered the new thirty-inch tables today and the rep for the new distributor stopped in to make sure the warehouse delivered on time."

A soft knock at the door interrupted their conversation, "Hey boss." Tasha served as the club's manager. She and Rolf had shared a long history. They had been lovers through the decades, but at this point they found themselves in a comfortable friendship. He knew that she sometimes still fed on the mortals, but only on the bad elements of society "It's been pretty quiet this evening. Not a bad crowd for a weeknight." The Elder, Thomas, turned her at seventeen She remained his captive for several years. Thomas was old school and believed women should remain in the convent. Things had changed while Thomas slept. The Elders were required to sleep for two hundred years in order to rejuvenate. It was almost time for him to awaken and Rolf was not looking forward to it. His relationship with Thomas was tense on their good days.

But, Armand, the current elder of the coven, would take his two-hundred-year hiatus when Thomas returned. He needed his rest but Rolf would miss him. It was Armand's wife, Lisette, who had turned him into a vampire.

Rolf headed home about an hour before sunrise. His home was dark and lonely. He went to the kitchen and fixed himself a night cap. He always kept the fridge stocked with food and drink just in case anyone stopped in to check. His housekeeper, Rosha, had been with him for thirty years. He hated to see her aging and in poor health. She wouldn't be with him for much longer. He'd offered to turn her, but she'd refused.

"I don't want to watch the people I love die," she'd reasoned. He very much understood her position, but he would miss her. She cooked him dinner every night, hoping that one day he would actually try it. He always sent the food home with her.

He couldn't put his finger on what was going on with him lately. There was an evil foreboding in the air. He suspected it was the influx of rouge vampires. They were brutal and merciless in their kills; they enjoyed turning the dregs of society into the worst of the night walkers. Rolf knew that the problems would only escalate once Thomas was awakened. He made his way up to his room and climbed into his coffin.

Chapter Three

Bellevue Hospital, New York City—Dr. Christine Rodgers was just arriving for her shift. She pulled her long blonde hair into a ponytail as she entered the hospital. A nationally recognized psychologist, she could have worked at any hospital in the country or enjoyed the benefits of a successful private practice, but she wanted to help the people who had no one else. Jeff, the registered nurse assigned to her ward, waited for her at the entrance.

"Well, Doc, we have a new patient. This one is a vampire—complete with fangs and everything. Says he was turned to serve a woman named Tristin. He has the trademark puncture wounds to prove it," Jeff shrugged. *It's going to be a long sixteen hours,* Christine thought. There were several new patients, but she was looking forward to seeing the vampire first. From early childhood, the underworld, with its vampires, werewolves and the like, fascinated her. After her parents were killed in a traffic accident, she relied heavily on her fantasy world. She had no one else left, but her work was her life; her life, her work.

She never went out socially. She had all of her meals delivered to her flat. The volume of her menu collection competed with that of her medical journals.

She entered the ward and proceeded down the hall. There were thirty rooms on this floor. The most recent intake was in the first room. Orderlies restrained the more reactionary patients before she entered their rooms. There were two with the victim at this time.

She examined the marks on the patient's neck. She was intrigued how they'd perfectly hit their mark. She tried talking to him with little response. But, as she turned to leave he wrestled out of the restraints with super-human effort and launched to attack her. Seasoned orderlies wrested him to the ground, giving him another injection, and then another before he calmed. Christine couldn't believe the amount of medication it required to knock him out. She had the orderly put him in a strait jacket and moved to another room.

Ten patients later, she heard the 'code blue' alarm ring through the halls. It was coming from the vampire's room. She chuckled to herself, *if her colleagues discovered her obsession with the undead, she would be the one locked up in a rubber room.* As she arrived at the door of the locked room, the orderly said that he went in to check on the patient and the patient was gone. The strait jacket reduced to a pile of ashes.

"Lock down the entire hospital immediately. And I want samples of that dust."

"Yes, Dr. Rodgers."

Two hours passed with no sign of the patient. No strangers had been allowed in or out of the hospital. Christine found herself reasoning that he must have just burned to death, spontaneous human combustion. There was no other reasonable explanation. There was absolutely no sign of fire besides the burned pile of clothing.

Chapter Four

As the evening sun began its decent Rolf awoke and went about his normal chores. As he sipped his vial of blood, there was a loud knock at the door. Before Rolf had the door fully opened Kyle pushed his way in.

"Rolf, something strange happened at the hospital today."

"What? What is it?"

"They admitted a vampire." Kyle exclaimed.

"Impossible."

"You heard me right. He was in a strait jacket and confined to a locked room, but when they went to check on him, he'd disappeared into thin air. All that remained was a pile of ash. The documentation states that he kept calling out for Tristin, claiming that she was his master."

"Did you say Tristin?"

"Yes, Rolf. Do you know her?"

"I did a long time ago. This can't be good for you mortals, or for vampires that don't kill for their food for that matter. She is what you call, 'hard-core old school." Rolf rushed over to the hospital and made his way to the isolation ward. Surprisingly, there weren't many people around, so it was easy for him to slip in. As he entered the ward, he could sense that the vampire was a bottom feeder. If he couldn't find any humans to feed on, he would settle for rat.

Just as Rolf was leaving the room, he ran smack into the woman from his dreams.

"What are you doing here?" Christine demanded, "This is a restricted area.".

"I…I'm the new orderly," he lied.

"May I see your badge?"

"Umm…I seemed to have lost it," Rolf fumbled around, searching his pockets.

"Security!" she called.

"I must have left it in my locker." Suddenly, there was a noise behind her. She turned to locate the source but when she turned back around, Rolf was nowhere to be found.

Chapter Five

Christine couldn't stop replaying the events of the evening in her mind. It felt like it had been straight out of a movie. The man who disappeared through locked doors had not been caught on any of the surveillance cameras. More than anything else, she couldn't get the image of his soulful eyes out of her mind. He looked at her as if he'd known her somehow. The stranger part was, she had felt the same way about him.

She arrived home just as the sun approached the eastern horizon. Rolf remained hidden as he watched her disappear into the foyer of her building. As the sun crept up over the mountain tops, he realized that he had better head home too before he ended up like the bottom feeder. Rolf climbed into his coffin but didn't feel the same sense of security. He had never felt this way before—not even when he was first turned. That moment had felt exciting to a young rouge. His mind went back to when he first saw Tristin. She was the most beautiful woman ever created. It was too bad that her beauty didn't extend below the surface. She was one of the few women that Thomas actually admired.

Tristin was livid when she heard about her newest subject's encounter at the hospital. It was hard to find a good slave nowadays. Society had changed so much in the last four hundred years. *Oh well*, she thought, *tonight I will find a replacement.* She had heard of a new vampire club that had just opened; rumor had it that it was run by an old friend. Her source told her that there were humans who frequented the club, actually believing that they were vampires. That would be the perfect place to find a willing participant in her game. Tristin's thoughts turned to Rolf. She remembered the first time they met. He had been one of the best lovers she'd ever had. She never could figure out when he had become so noble as to feed off blood from a bag. *To each his own...* she rolled her eyes.

She'd run into Rolf three hundred years ago. He was on a field of honor somewhere in Europe; a lord of the realm had caught him in bed with his wife. Rolf had sensed her, another vampire, and took his eyes off of his opponent. The was the instant the irate husband needed, he shot Rolf through the heart. Tristin had gone to the morgue before they came for him. She made a small cut in her wrist and fed him her blood. He awoke with a start, believing that this woman had saved him. He thought it had been love at first sight, but it didn't take long for Rolf to realize that he was very wrong. He had run into her several times over the years, and the encounters always ended in bed. Then, he'd vanish as fast as he could—putting continents between them.

Chapter Six

Christine made her way through the busy sidewalks of Manhattan. She was deep in thought, unaware of the man following her—he blended well with the shadows. Rolf's growing obsession with Christine played havoc with common sense. She was definitely the woman he had been dreaming about. This was the third night in a row that he had been following her. Strangely, he was beginning to feel protective of her. If he was drawn to her, that meant others would be as well, and he was not going to let that happen.

Christine was on her way to the hospital. She had traded shifts with another doctor so that she could be on hand if any additional bizarre cases found their way in. As she continued her walk, she couldn't shake the feeling that she was being watched. She changed her route just in case. Even though it was a little creepy feeling like there were eyes on her, she had the sense that she was protected, not in danger. When she arrived at work, the orderly told her that there wasn't any new information on the missing vampire case. It was otherwise a very quiet night at the hospital.

The same could not be said at the city morgue. Two bodies had turned up with their blood completely drained. There was also a body missing.

The coroner made notes in his shift report, while across town, Christine read over what was being documented. *Fascinating*, she thought. She pulled up reports from other coroners and found more cases that matched. She took a cab across town, but by the time she arrived, another body had disappeared without a trace. There was no sign of it besides a pile of ash and burnt clothing. Again, the surveillance tapes were monitored and there was no evidence of anyone coming in or out—or anything suspicious for that matter.

Chapter Seven

Rolf was in a cab on the way to the club. He had received a 9-1-1 call from William and Tasha. His valet opened the door of the cab and cleared a path for him into the club. It was a very busy night for a Tuesday. He headed straight for his office with William following right on his heels. Rolf had noticed a few new vampires in the club this evening, along with a couple of slaves who hadn't been fully turned yet. Tasha came in and confirmed that the John Does had been at the club. One was found inside, so they moved him two blocks down and left him in an alleyway.

"Has there been any sign of Tristin?" Rolf asked, almost dreading the answer.

"No," both William and Tasha answered simultaneously.

"Well, let stay alert. This is very much her MO, and I wouldn't be surprised to find out she's nearby. I can feel her everywhere. I need to find her before the awakening."

"Of course, Rolf." William said, returning to the hustle and bustle of the front room. Tasha stayed behind.

"How are you doing Rolf?" she asked. Before he could answer, Kyle appeared in the doorway.

"What's going on? You never come to the club," Rolf asked surprised.

"I haven't seen you in two nights!"

"I'm fine, Kyle. I found the woman in my dreams and I've been following her."

"Really?"

"Yes, she's a doctor at Bellevue. Dr. Christine Rodgers. Do you know her?"

"Yes, of course. She's one of the best in her field. Rolf, she's been going all over town trying to find clues to all the deaths that have been occurring. All of these bodies turning up with their blood drained has raised quite a bit of suspicion."

"How many have there been?"

"Four at last count. I brought your injection."

"Thank you, Kyle."

"So, what are you going to do now?"

"All I can do for now is wait. If Tristin doesn't want to be found, she won't be. What worries me is that it's only a few weeks until the awakening, and there could be a bloodbath."

"I need to get back to the hospital, but we'll talk more about this later."

"See you later tonight. And Kyle, be careful. These are not like any vampire you have ever met before."

"Of course, Rolf. I'll be careful."

Christine had had a restless night of sleep. She was having a hard time adjusting to working the night shift, but she was sure there would be more deaths to come. She was frustrated that she still hadn't received the test results from the pile of ashes from the first patient. If she didn't get them back soon, she was ready to test them herself. She attempted a few more hours of rest before her shift. She fell into a very vivid dream about a monster who would turn into a human. This man was terrifying. He had a circle of men and women in dark robes around him, praying. In the middle, stood the most beautiful woman on Earth. Christine woke up the instant that the woman made eye contact with her. She sat up straight in her bed with cold sweat running down her spine. She no longer felt the desire to fight for sleep.

When Christine returned to the hospital she found total chaos. They were dealing with a new patient who had already put two orderlies twice his size in the ER. All of this after they had given him enough drugs to knock out a horse—a very large horse. She cautiously entered the exam room and noticed that he too had bite marks, just as the other man had. He also kept calling for Tristin.

"The time is near! The time is near!" he would scream over and over again. Taking her notes, she continued with her rounds pondering what he could mean. Around four o'clock in the morning, a shrill alarm filled the halls once again. A creepy sense of Deja vu washed over Christine as she walked toward the room. When she arrived, she was stunned by the site inside the room. She immediately put a hand to her mouth to muffle her scream and she torn her eyes away from the patient. She slowly was able to look at him again. The man was lying there, not a drop of blood spilled, with a large stake through his heart. The orderlies confirmed that no one had had access to the room besides them. Security was called and they immediately placed the ward on lock-down.

"Get the coroner in here asap! No one is allowed in this room until this patient is examined by the coroner. Understand?" Christine barked.

As soon as the coroner arrived she led him into the sealed room. As before, only ashes and charred clothing remained. "Impossible!" she muttered to herself. She ran to the security office and reviewed the tapes—nothing. Her mind reeled with a myriad of questions no one could answer.

Around seven o'clock that morning, she left for home. As she walked, she remembered the dream she had the night before. *It seemed so real,* she thought. Almost as if she had lived it herself. Instead of going home, she headed in the direction of a used bookstore she had been meaning to visit. The store was in an old building in a quieter part of the city. It was dark inside, and although it seemed clean, a musty smell lingered throughout the stacks. The man behind the counter looked even older than the building.

Christine made her way to the back of the store and found a section on rituals. It took her over an hour to find one that matched the what she saw in her dream. This particular ritual dated back thousands of years. She carried the book to the counter, paid the clerk, and took it home for further study.

It turned dark and dreary as a storm moved in from the southwest. Christine lunged into a cab just as the rain hit. It was after eleven by the time she made it home. Exhausted and able to find a quiet place in her mind she dropped off to sleep quickly.

Chapter Eight

Compared to her last shift, tonight was a really slow night. She decided to take a break and walk to the corner coffee shop. She ordered two coffees, then walked back; all the while acutely aware that she was being watched. She noticed a man in dark clothing walking about a thousand feet behind her. Christine thought he looked familiar, but it was hard to tell because he was so far away.

She arrived back at the hospital just in time for her rounds. Suddenly, a shadow at the far window caught her eye. She called security to go and check it out; everything was clear. *Stop being so paranoid*, she scolded herself. Jeff, her nurse, found her in the last patient's room.

"Doctor, you asked me to let you know if any other strange events happen. St. Marks just had one come in with bite marks."

"Thank you, Jeff. I'll go over there as soon as I can."

"What do you think is going on, Doc?"

"I wish I knew. Maybe a serial killer?"

Rolf was making his way back to his Brownstone. He had spent most of the night watching Dr. Rodgers. Even though he was glad that he finally figured out who she was, he still didn't know why he was dreaming of her. He stood on the porch, poised to unlock the door when he sensed a presence, her presence.

"Alright Tristin, come on out." As shadow gracefully flew down from a high reaching tree and landed before him.

"Rolf, it's been so long. I'm glad to see you are still in touch with yourself. Don't you miss the hunt and kill at least a little bit?"

"No…I don't. What do you want?"

"Just visiting an old friend," she purred with a dangerous grin.

"You better get back to your place. It'll be light soon. I'm still working on the cure against sunshine."

"When are you going to give up on all this Rolf? Embrace your destiny. Thomas won't be as easy on you and you know it."

"Worry about yourself and leave me alone." She laughed at his dismissive attitude and disappeared into what was left of the night. Rolf thought to himself, *how could I have been so in love with such a monster?* After letting himself into the house, he drank a glass of blood and retired to his coffin.

Chapter Nine

Across town, Dr. Rodgers was having another nightmare. This time, during the ritual, a woman emerged from behind a closed door drenched in blood. She entered the space and joined the ritual, standing just to the left of the monster and the beautiful woman. Christine suddenly awoke from the dream. She dressed for the night shift and left a little early—wanting to be sure that she had enough time to stop by St. Marks. The storm outside was relentless, so she had the doorman call her a cab.

She arrived at St. Marks and went straight down to the morgue. She shivered perceptively and knew more than damp, stormy air caused her discomfort.

"How can I help you Dr. Rodgers?"

"I would like to see your reports on the John Doe who came in with puncture wounds on his neck."

"Of course, Doctor. I'll go get them. There's coffee in the breakroom if you're interested."

"Thank you." She was interested. She grabbed herself a Styrofoam cup and returned to the front desk. It was probably the worst cup of coffee she had ever had, but she was grateful for the warmth. Once the attendant returned with the file, she scanned it quickly, then asked to see the body. The attendant took her to the freezer, opened the drawer, and found it completely empty. The body was gone. No ashes, no clothing, just empty.

Kyle knocked on Rolf's door. It was several minutes before the housekeeper answered. She told him that he could go on up and see Rolf.

"Rolf, good evening."

"Is it Kyle?"

"No...not really. Another body with puncture wounds was found. I followed the good doctor to St. Marks, and this one was very different."

"In what way?"

"The body was gone. No ashes, no clothing."

"What? Tristin never leaves them alive unless they are her personal slave. I believe the first one was hers already."

"So, what do you think is going on?"

"I'll let you know tonight."

"Well, I brought your blood. I'm think I'm going to call it a night."

"Thank you...for everything Kyle."

"Oh, you know I love all of the intrigue; besides, if I tried telling anyone else, the good doctor would have a really nice room for me."

"Good night Kyle."

"Same Rolf." After Kyle was gone, Rolf went downstairs and told his housekeeper to pack up and go home to her family.

"Of course, sir. See you tomorrow." Rolf's mind could only think of the missing body. He knew that this was not Tristin's style. If she turned someone, it was because she wanted them to stay with her. He had no doubt that the others were hers; but this one just didn't fit. He made his way over to the club, and again, it was packed. He mingled with a few of the patrons, then went to the office. It wasn't long before William joined him.

"Any new vampires here tonight?" he asked William.

"Not that I've noticed so far, sir."

"Please keep your eyes open for anyone new. It's important."

"Of course, see you tomorrow" William left Rolf looking over the previous evening's take. Rolf struggled to keep his mind focused. He couldn't stop thinking about Christine and the case at St. Marks. There was a bad feeling in the pit of his stomach that he couldn't explain.

Chapter Ten

Christine perused her book of rituals during her lunch break. Engrossed in the subject, she didn't notice the orderly who approached her until he spoke.

"Doctor, another patient has arrived with puncture wounds."

"I'll be right there." She jumped up and stashed her belongings into her locker. She hurried to the isolation ward and entered the most recent victim's room. He was so agitated he seemed completely unaware of the people surrounding him. He wasn't making any sense, and she realized that he was speaking language she had never heard before. She planned to keep a very close eye on this one. She asked two guards to join her in monitoring him for the rest of the night. No one was allowed in besides herself and her orderly.

Two hours before daylight, the man woke up fighting his bonds. The orderly ordered the guard to find Dr. Rodgers stat. He was preparing the injection when the lights flashed out. He could barely see the needle in his hand. He blinked his eyes a couple to times to allow them to adjust to the darkness. He thought he saw the outline of a tall, thin woman. She was too tall to be Dr. Rodgers. Besides, he knew she was the only woman on staff that night. Before he could administer the injection, the woman flew toward him and sunk her teeth into the side of his neck. The orderly could feel the life slowly leaving his body. After sucking him dry of blood she attacked and drained the patient. She left the two men dead on the floor.

Christine arrived in the doorway of the locked room and was shocked by the brutality before her. The victims' bodies sprawled lifelessly on the floor, their necks laid open yet only a trace of blood stained the scene. She turned, sickened and shocked by what she saw, and left the room.

Rolf watched from the shadows. He knew this wasn't Tristin's work because she was currently sitting in his club. He'd called to verify. He watched as people came, viewed the gruesome scene, and left. The guards came out white as a ghost, one of them heaved right in the hallway. Rolf could hear Christine speaking to the coroner on the phone. He was sending up an assistant to retrieve the bodies. He assured her that we would conduct the autopsy himself and send the results to her as soon as he was able.

Rolf waited until everyone left the before he slid into the locked room. He stood quietly amid the carnage. Unable to sense who butchered the victims, he assumed it must be the work of an Elder. He couldn't bring to mind anyone who wrecked such havoc in modern times. He felt she must be three or four thousand years old.

He heard a key in the door and moved into the shadows. Christine entered and stood quietly surveying the grizzly scene. Even without the copious amount of blood one would expect it was a gruesome sight. She looked around a bit didn't find anything to help her envision what had happened and with a perplexed shake of her head she returned to her office to wait for the police.

Rolf waited quietly while the officers and investigators did their work. Once the scene was cleared the assistant removed the bodies. Christine finished her rounds and returned to her office. She found it hard to focus on her paperwork as pictures of the mangled bodies flashed across her mind. A knock on her door startled her. Before she could look up the door had opened and two homicide detectives let themselves in. "Why have the bodies already been moved?" demanded the older, red-faced detective. He approached Christine's desk, placed his fists on it and leaned heavily on his knuckles. His face only inches from her he cursed and ordered, "Answer me, immediately."

Christine calmly pushed herself away from her desk, "We were told they were through and we could move the bodies. We wanted them out of there as quickly as possible to prevent anyone else from seeing them. She stood, walked around her desk, stopped only inches from the detective who'd so rudely entered her space. "The patients on this floor are in fragile states to begin with. To be exposed to such heinous confusion would probably set them back, maybe never to be reached again. You," she emphasized, "will find your corpses in the morgue." She stood there, unyielding, until Rudy (she'd mentally named him) made a move to leave. The younger detective, who'd stood off to the side during her tirade, eyes bulging, heart pounding moved to open the door for his senior and hurried after him without a word.

Christine followed them to the crime scene. Rudy waited quietly while she unlocked the door. He stepped inside and paused, hands on his hips. He looked around the room, "How is it they got all the blood cleaned up but didn't put the rest of the room to order? I am assuming all this equipment lying about was flung about during the crime."

Christine paused a moment and then quietly offered, "There was no blood."

Not knowing how to respond Rudy turned and walked out the door, "Let's go to the morgue."

Christine locked the door and led the detectives to the morgue, *I'll be glad to turn these guys over to Grant.*, "Grant," she hollered, "I've got some detectives here that want to see your bodies." She looked around but the ME was not in the room. The tables where the remains should be were oddly pristine. Rudy was opening each cold locker, his partner followed behind, closing them. After five or six opened doors Rudy shouted, "Where are they!"

Christine, although not surprised, had no answer for him. Rudy spoke to his partner as they inspected the last locker, "It's looks like we have another crime scene here. Stolen bodies, dead ones. Shut this place down. No one in or out."

Christine returned to her office, *It's going to be a long night* she sighed as she opened her office door. She stopped short. She hadn't been gone that long, yet her book of rituals lay opened on her desk. She approached her desk cautiously, not knowing if someone would jump from behind it. She quickly noticed the book lay opened to where she'd left off. She knew, without a doubt, she hadn't left it there. In fact, she remembered very clearly putting it in her locker. The ritual being described was over five thousand years old. It detailed an evil rising to make Earth a dark place, similar to hell—a place where only it could reside. Christine felt a shiver travel down her back as she read on. She turned the page and came face to face with a photo of the monster from her dream. There was a strange language written at the bottom of the photo. She wished she understood what the words meant. She closed the book and locked it in her desk. She picked up her reports and went to turn them in for the daytime staff. By the time she was done, the police had lifted the lockdown, and she was allowed to go home.

Chapter Eleven

Rolf felt totally out of touch. Kyle arrived, his worry evident.

"What's happened now?" Rolf asked.

"I overheard some detectives talking at the hospital last night, about Dr. Rodgers. They are suspicious that she is always on shift when these murders and disappearances are taking place."

"I wish there was some way to keep her out of this, but it's too late now. Find Pete and Rachel for me. I want people watching her at all times."

"Of course, Rolf. I'll stop by later." Kyle left to do his friend this favor. Rolf finished a vile of blood and went upstairs to rest. He couldn't stop thinking about the sheer brutality of those attacks. Whoever was doing this was very powerful, and very, very dangerous.

Rolf dreamt of the night he was turned into a vampire. He'd married the lovely and engaging Elizabeth that afternoon. Following a day of festivities, they headed back to the castle for the night. Darkness fell long before they reached the castle. However, he'd spotted the lights in the distance as they approached so he held no concern and quietly discussed the events of the day with his new bride. Out of nowhere, three dark figures descended upon them. Rolf tried everything within his power to save Elizabeth, but the attackers were too strong and fierce. He could only watch a woman grab her and sink frightfully sharp fangs into Elizabeth's neck. The last thing he saw was her eyes turning black before he lost consciousness He woke in a very dark room. He didn't know how he had gotten there, or where he was. He stood up and walked over to the window. He tried the door, but it was locked. He yelled for help until his throat was raw, and exhaustion overtook him.

When he woke again, there was a nicely dressed man in the room with him. *He must be wealthy to afford such clothing*, Rolf remembered thinking. The man only stared at him for what felt like hours before he finally spoke.

"Do you understand what happened, Rolf?"

"No. Where is my wife?"

"My apologies, but she didn't make it through the change."

"What change?"

"Rolf, you are now going to be a part of my family. We don't die like the mortals do. There are ways that we can die, but you won't have to worry about that. You can't walk in the daylight or you will burn. For now, get some rest. You will learn how to feed tonight."

Rolf jumped awake. He hadn't had that dream for quite some time. He remained contemplative as he went through routine tasks and waited for Kyle to arrive.

"Good day Kyle."

"Same to you."

"Any new problems I should be aware of?"

"Not yet. I have eyes trailing Christine."

"Thank you, Kyle."

"Have you figured out why you keep dreaming of her?"

"No, but I know it all fits, somehow."

"Yes, I agree."

"Well, I'm on my way to see my old friend Victor. I'm hoping he'll be able to shed some light on what's been happening. I'll see you later tonight." Kyle simply nodded in acknowledgment before they departed.

Rolf arrived at Victor's residence. The butler informed him that Victor was out of the country until the next day. Rolf thanked him and headed to the club.

Tasha met him at the bottom of the stairs "Hey boss," she smiled, "It's a quiet night, there's only a small crowd." William was on his way across the room with a bottle and a chilled glass for Rolf.

"The books are on your desk," William said handing him the bottle and glass.

"Thank you, William." Judging by the books, the club was doing extremely well. New York was a tough place to start a business, let alone a club for vampires.

Chapter Twelve

Christine was relieved to have a slow night. She was very behind on her paperwork. She thought it would be nice to just get it all out of the way. Unfortunately, the quiet wouldn't last. Around two o'clock in the morning, the EMTs brought a young woman in with bite marks on the side of her neck. Judging by the looks of her, she was most likely a homeless person. She had track marks all over her arms. When she finally calmed down, and was secured to the bed, they left her alone to get on with the rest of their rounds. Come four-thirty, all was still in the ward. Christine went to go check on Jane Doe, shocked to still see her there, resting.

She made it home before she realized her ritual book was still locked inside her desk. She wished she would have thought to bring it with her, but she didn't feel up to going back to the hospital. She set her alarm so she would have time to go back to the bookstore before her next shift.

The next afternoon, as she enjoyed her coffee, she realized she hadn't had a dream. After a week of non-stop dreaming, it felt strange, it had just stopped. She called down and asked the valet to call a cab. As soon as she stepped outside, she sensed she had a watcher again. She looked around, but again, noticed nothing out of the ordinary. She gave the cabby the address to the bookstore and sat back to catch up on some text messages that she needed to respond to. Traffic was at a standstill, so she didn't arrive at the bookstore until fifteen minutes before six. She walked up to the storefront and was shocked to see an 'out of business' sign hanging in the window.

She went into the store next door and found an eightyish woman dusting shelves, "When did the bookstore go out of business?" she smiled.

"Oh honey, that old store has been gone for at least thirty years now."

"Are…are you sure?"

"Little lady, I may be old, but I'm still sharp as a tack. I'm sure." Pete and Rachel sat across the street watching the exchange but couldn't tell what was going on. After Christine left, Pete went in and asked the clerk what the young lady had been inquiring about. He was happy Christine was on foot now; she would be easier to keep up with. He called Kyle to fill him in on the events so far. Kyle was already on his way to meet Rolf when he received the phone call.

Rolf had not slept well. He felt extremely restless and couldn't put his finger on the reason. He had just finished his second glass of blood when he heard a knock at the door. He was surprised to hear the knock a second time as he had made his way to the entrance.

"Where is Rosha? She is always here before I am," Kyle asked.

"In the last thirty years, she has never been late or sick." Rolf attempted to call her cell phone. The call went straight to voicemail. "Kyle, will you go and check on her. Please? I've got an appointment with Victor. Call me as soon as you can."

"Of course."

Victor had finally returned from his travels. Rolf filled him in on the events that happened while he was away. When he showed him some of the crime-scene photos, Victor blanched at the grizzly scenes.

"Rolf, let me get my bearings on this okay? Give me a few days."

"Of course. Welcome home my friend. Where is your lovely wife?"

"Charlotte will be here in a few days. It has been a long time since we have been together." Rolf felt uneasy by Victor's reaction to the photos, but he knew that you couldn't rush an Elder. Rolf bid Victor goodbye and went to the club. Instead of going to his office first, he went straight to the bar. William appeared with a glass and a bottle as soon as Rolf sat down.

"What's wrong, chief?"

"I've just got an uneasy feeling. How's it going tonight?"

"Nice and steady."

"Any new vampires?"

"Not tonight chief. Just the usual crowd." Rolf downed two drinks before making his way up to the office.

Chapter Thirteen

Kyle came rushing up the stairs and beat on Rolf's door. He was disheveled and talking so fast that he wasn't making any sense at all. Rolf poured him two fingers of brandy to help him calm down.

"Rolf, they're all dead!"

"Calm down, who's all dead?"

"Rosha, her entire family. It was a blood bath. I couldn't get close enough, but what I did see turned my blood cold. Their necks were ripped out. Blood everywhere!"

"William! Get me my car... now!"

"Of course, chief, right away."

By the time Rolf arrived at the residence, there were cops everywhere. EMTs checked for the possibility of survivors and CSIs processed the scene. They wouldn't allow him to come close, but he was able to hear everything. There was no evidence or DNA anywhere in the house. The detectives on the scene were the same two who had reported to the hospital. *It has to be a vampire. No mortal could be this vicious.* He had a feeling that, even though this was related to the other killings, it wasn't done by the same killer. He knew that Rosha didn't have any enemies. Rolf walked up to the yellow tape.

"Excuse me, officer. I need to speak to whoever is in charge here."

"Why?"

"Because this is my housekeeper's home."

"Wait here." Another officer approached him.

"You are going to have to wait until I'm able to speak with you. Stick around." The officer in charge instructed. Rolf agreed and stayed back so that he could observe the crowd. When they were finally able to talk to him, the first question they asked was, "Why are you here?"

"She's been my housekeeper for thirty years and has never been late or sick. I knew as soon as she didn't show up today that something was wrong."

"Okay, thank you. Here's my card. Call me if you can think of anything else." Rolf took the card and hurried home to beat the rising sun. He made it inside and got the drapes closed just in time. He sat down to think, even though he knew that he needed to rejuvenate. His sleep patterns had been so off the last couple of nights. He was able to get some rest for a little while…then the dreams started.

It felt so real. The woman in this dream was slim and tall for a woman. Her raven black hair fell below her waist. When she turned to face him, her eyes shone an eerie gold. He felt an unrelenting draw to her and was about to fold her in his arms when Christine suddenly grabbed his arm. He jumped back into consciousness and suddenly became aware of a pounding on the door.

"Same dream?" Kyle could tell by the look on Rolf's face that it had been a doozy.

"No, this one had a different woman in it. Any more bad news?"

"No, it's been quiet. Still no trace of the vampire who's been doing this. I have every watcher on the lookout. I'm so sorry about Rosha and her family. It's like it was a personal vendetta against you."

"Hmmm, I hadn't thought of it like that. You may be right."

"Oh! Come to think of it, there was a strange incident. A woman was admitted into Bellevue with two puncture wounds, but she's still there. She hasn't disappeared or burned up like the others. Dr. Rodgers is off tonight and tomorrow night."

"Anything else on the new vic?"

"Well, she was pretty dirty when they brought her in, and she had track marks on her arms and feet. They tagged her as a Jane Doe."

"I'm going to go over there now. Is someone with Christine?"

"I have a team with her around the clock."

"Good. Get some rest Kyle."

"See you later."

"Be careful my friend."

Chapter Fourteen

Christine just couldn't wrap her brain around what had happened at the bookstore. *How could it be closed? I was just there.* She had gone back twice just to make sure she hadn't imagined it. She hadn't slept at all the night before, and she was not looking forward to the night ahead. After hours of tossing and turning, she got up and called for a cab. She checked in with the guards at the hospital to make sure that everything was going well before going to her office. She hoped she wouldn't have to explain to anyone why she was there.

She unlocked the door to her office and was stunned to see that it had been completely ransacked. There were books all over the floor, papers everywhere, her desk was on its side, and the only drawer that hadn't been opened was the one that contained the rituals book. She immediately called for security, but nobody could explain what took place in her office. She asked that they call the police. As soon as she was alone, she retrieved the book and put it in her bag. She ran out of the hospital, hailed a cab, and gave him her address. When she arrived back at her building, something struck her about the doorman. She didn't get a good look at his face, but he felt familiar for some reason. *He must be new*, she thought. She bid him a polite goodnight, but he just nodded in response. When she reached her floor, she noticed an elderly woman walking toward her. As the woman neared, a tall dark shadow stepped out from the shadows. The old woman turned to walk away, and in the blink of an eye, they both disappeared

She opened her front door and gasped. Her apartment was in ruin, just as her office had been. She called down for the security guard and asked them to inform the police. She gave her statement to an officer who instructed that she would have to go inside to wait for the detective.

Rolf watched from an empty room across the street. It seemed like an eternity before the police finally left. He could see Christine through an open window. She was busy putting things back in their place. He couldn't stick around for much longer; it would be daylight soon. She seemed to sense him, even if she wasn't directly aware of it. Before he left, he noticed one of Kyle's friends taking a similar vantage point. She was as safe as she could be. When he got home, he noticed an unmarked police car parked out front. The detectives told him that they needed to follow up on Rosha.

"Of course, please come in." He hoped this wouldn't take long. It had been hours since his last feeding. He found it hard to concentrate on their questions when he could hear the blood pumping through their veins.

"Do you know if she has any other family?"

"I'm not sure."

"Well, if we don't find someone to claim the bodies, they are all going to Potter's Field." Rolf felt his anger surge at the way they were talking about Rosha. "Don't leave town, okay friend?"

"You had better catch their killer before I do," Rolf threatened. The officers only nodded and walked out of the house. Rolf rushed for the refrigerator that kept his precious blood supply hidden. He didn't even bother with a glass. Having gotten his fill, he let his body fall into a nearby chair. The house felt so empty without Rosha. He thought back on their time together over the last thirty years and about how special she had been to him. He suddenly grew nauseous, feeling as though he was somehow responsible for her grisly death. No one deserved what she went through. He called the detectives and let them know that he would come down and claim the bodies. Kyle showed up a little while later with a fresh blood supply and offered to help with the funeral arrangements.

That morning, Rolf dreamt he was watching someone tearing Rosha's children apart, one by one. They killed Rosha last, after she had watched the rest of her family perish.

Chapter Fifteen

Christine couldn't stay at her apartment; it was just too unsettling. She thought about going back to the hospital, but the police were probably still there. She went downstairs and looked around for the doorman. *He must be on his inspection rounds*, she thought. Several police cars had been parked in front of the building. She asked one of the officers if he had seen the doorman or knew when he'd be back.

"There was no one here when we arrived, miss," he told her. *That's odd*...she thought. She was able to grab a cab herself and asked him to take her to the Roosevelt Hotel. Christine paid the cabby and checked into the hotel. She went to her room, took a few minutes to settle in, and ordered some breakfast. She was too tired to eat most of the meal. She was pretty sure that she had fallen asleep before her head even hit the pillow.

She dreamt of wolves and bats. Then, she saw an altar. Upon closer look, she noticed that it was her body laying at the altar. She bolted out of bed, drenched in sweat. She thought her heart was going to beat right out of her chest. She took a few deep breaths as she became acquainted with her surroundings. She realized that she had slept well into mid-morning. She ordered some lunch and hopped in the shower. Feeling a little more refreshed, she returned to her apartment. She focused her attention on getting a few more things put away, then settled down on the couch to read. She fell asleep almost immediately with the book in her lap.

When she awoke, she noticed that it had started to rain again. *This weather has been nuts for the last few weeks*, she thought to herself. She got herself up and ready for work. When she arrived, an orderly told her about a massacre that had occurred at his building.

"They were torn apart, Doc. All of them. The youngest was four or five years old."

"Where did they take the bodies?" she asked.

"St. Marks."

"Could you please get me the number for the coroner over there?"

"Of course, Doc."

Well isn't this a great start to the night, she thought. She had ten new patients to check in and evaluate on top of her normal patients. She had no time to read at all, but she kept the book with her, in her bag. She knew that, somehow, it was connected to her dreams and to the chain of recent deaths.

It was still an hour before daylight, so Rolf made his way down to the morgue. They took him straight back to the viewing room, where he signed all of the necessary paperwork. Once everything had been taken care of, he walked out of the room and literally ran into Christine. He grabbed her to keep her from falling. When she looked up at him, she immediately recognized those soulful eyes.

"You! What are you doing here? Are you, like, stalking me or something?"

"I believe I was here first."

"What are you doing here?"

"My housekeeper and her family were killed last night."

"The family of five...yes, my orderly lived across from them. I'm so sorry for your loss."

"I'm Rolf. I'm truly sorry, but I must rush off."

"Do you mind if I examine the bodies?"

"Would I really stop you if I said yes?"

"No," she laughed. "Have a good day."

"Doctor," he nodded before walking off. He was kicking himself as he hurried home. This was the second night that he was almost caught by the sunlight. He would have to be more careful. He found message from Victor when he got home, asking if they could meet the next evening.

Chapter Sixteen

Rolf awoke promptly at sunset the next night. He went straight for his blood supply, thinking his feelings of unease were the result of his thirst. He was anxious about what Victor would have to say. As he approached Victor's residence, the front door opened before he could even knock.

"Rolf, I am afraid that someone wants to wake the queen. What do you know of her?"

"I was told that she was a myth."

"Afraid not. Five thousand years ago, she was taken to a tomb in the mountains somewhere in Eastern Europe. Once it was discovered she was both vampire and werewolf the Elders of the time feared she had too much power. She was poisoned and locked in a tomb for all eternity. They say that you could hear her screams for centuries afterward. Her parents were banished from their respective covens."

"How would anyone be able to trace her, Victor?"

"I was turned right after she was entombed. If anyone knows how to find and wake her, it's Thomas or Marco."

"But, they are both still asleep. Victor, you know that Tristin is here in New York, don't you?

"Yes, Charlotte told me. She wasn't happy to see her. I wasn't either."

"Nor I," Rolf scowled.

"We really need to find out what's going on. Do you still have those watcher friends of yours?"

"Of course. I will get them right on it."

"Keep me informed."

"Of course, Victor."

Charlotte came out just after Rolf left, "What's wrong darling? Don't you trust Rolf?"

"Of course, I do. It's just best, right now, to leave some things unsaid."

"You don't think that Rolf is being honest…"

"Don't get me wrong, I trust him with my life—as do you—but I saw something in his eyes tonight that I've never seen before." Charlotte disappeared and returned to the patio with a bottle and a couple of glasses "My love, do you ever miss the hunt and kill?" he asked.

"Yes, my dear, I do. But, I don't miss having people chasing us all the time."

Rolf went straight to the club after leaving Victor's. He stood at the bar as William poured him a drink.

"Anything new?"

"Not tonight chief."

"Thank-you, William." Rolf scanned the club again. "Where is Tasha?"

"She sent a text saying that she would be in later."

"And you didn't think that was strange?"

"I…uh…no. Sorry Rolf."

"Call me as soon as she gets here. I'm going to the hospital." Traffic was so congested he actually considered flying the rest of the way, *Nah, that's too risky.* Finally arriving at the hospital, Rolf asked the guard if Christine Rogers was on duty. She came to the gate as soon as she heard the page wondering who might be looking for her.

"You again," she said.

"Yes, the city morgue told me that you had the bodies of the murdered family brought here."

"I did…they are similar to some other cases I have been working on.

"She was my housekeeper, her family like my own. When do you anticipate releasing them? I'd like to see that they are properly buried."

"Come back in the morning. I should have all of the paperwork done by then."

"I'll have to send a friend. I have an early appointment."

"How long did she work for you?"

"Thirty years."

"I am so truly sorry for your loss. What is your name again?"

"Rolf. Rolf Rainey. I'm sure I will see you again Dr. Rodgers. Goodnight."

"Christine, please," she smiled, "You too, have a good night Rolf."

As soon as he left the building, he sensed another vampire nearby. He wasn't surprised to see Tristin emerge from the shadows.

"What is so special about this place anyway?" she asked.

"Not that it's any of your concern, but my house keeper and her family were murdered. You wouldn't happen to know anything about that would you?"

"Of course not, darling. Good evening, Rolf," she laughed as she flew away into the night. There was a feeling deep in the pit of his stomach that she was involved. He just knew it, but he needed more information. Rolf arrived at home and filled Kyle in on all he'd learned.

"You seem especially anxious tonight, Rolf."

"I've just got a terrible feeling about all of this. Be safe."

Chapter Seventeen

Christine's shift ran over; five new patients came in at the last minute. She left instructions to release Rosha and her relatives to Rolf. Her head was still spinning; she had never seen such brutality. When she arrived at home, she fixed herself a light breakfast, took a quick shower, and fell into a deep and peaceful sleep. It was her first decent rest in weeks.

Christine woke up refreshed and ready to face another night shift. She just had to make it through one more shift and then she would be able to enjoy three days off. She stepped out of the elevator into chaos. She paused, it became evident that the rogue vampires had been busy.

At his Brownstone Rolf received a call from Kyle, "Rolf, there is a woman being admitted into Bellevue as we speak. She had bite marks on her neck, but she's not a homeless person like the last one. She's from a very prominent family in the Hamptons."

"Is Dr. Rodgers on shift tonight?"

"She just arrived."

"Don't let her out of your sight Kyle. I'll be there soon. Be careful."

When Rolf arrived at the hospital, it was media bedlam. Newspaper and TV reporters swarmed the entrance. Rolf knew this would not bode well for his kind. It could start a whole new war against vampires. He stayed hidden in the shadows, listening to the media broadcasts. Suddenly, Dr. Rodgers stepped out of the hospital and addressed the eager reporters.

"The patient is resting. Yes, she has puncture wounds on her neck that appear to be bite marks, but she isn't in any danger at the moment. I would appreciate if you would all just go back to your work and let me focus on the care of my patient. I'll have a statement ready as soon as I have more answers. Thank you." She subtly scanned the crowd, hoping to see Rolf—she almost felt as if she could sense him near her.

Curious, Christine thought as she went back into the hospital. This was the second victim who hadn't caught fire—and another woman at that. She went to make sure that the patient was still resting. Carefully, she opened the door and was relieved to see the woman sound asleep. Christine finished her rounds and checked on the patient one last time before she clocked out for the evening. She wanted to make sure that all of the loose ends to neatly tied before her three days away from it all. When the doors shut behind her as she left the building she heard, mentally, a heavy metal clanging, keys locking and chains binding, as she swore to leave all the madness behind for three peace-filled days.

When she got home, she looked through all of her menus before deciding on her favorite pizza place. Okay, maybe it wasn't her favorite, but it was the only one that delivered twenty-four hours a day. Once her meal arrived, she opened up a bottle of wine, grabbed her book and settled in on the couch. As usual, it was only a matter of minutes before sleep overcame her. She awoke about two hours later with a stiff neck, so she ran a hot bubble bath. Once she finally ended up in bed, she slept for a solid fourteen hours straight.

She laid in bed for a little while the next morning, checking her voicemails. There was nothing important until she reached the last one. It was one of her colleagues from the hospital; the prominent Jane Doe had disappeared during the night. She called the hospital immediately to find out what was going on. The orderly told her that there was no sign of foul play, but again, nothing appeared on the security footage. She strongly considered going down to the hospital but was able to talk herself out of it.

She tossed a couple of pieces of leftover pizza on a plate and sat down to look at her long-neglected personal business. She pushed through her paperwork until she realized that she had forgotten about the pizza. As hard as she tried to concentrate, her mind kept wandering to the mysterious Rolf Rainey.

Rolf had gone to the hospital looking for Dr. Rodgers. The orderly told him that she wouldn't be for a couple of days. Rolf thanked him for the information. As he was leaving, he overheard someone saying that the socialite had vanished without a trace. He immediately got Kyle on the phone and asked him to check with his watchers to see if there were any more pieces to the puzzle.

"I'll let you know what I find out."

"Be careful Kyle."

"Same to you brother."

Rolf jumped onto the fire escape outside Christine's apartment. He made his way over to view inside her apartment. He saw her sitting on the couch, reading. The book was entitled, *Ancient Cults and Rituals*. He could tell, just by the look of it, that the book was centuries old. He could feel the energy radiating from it. He knew he had to get it away from her. Christine suddenly felt the hairs on the back of her neck stand on end. She knew she was being watched. She tried to tell herself that she was paranoid and burnt out from working so many strenuous shifts, but something told her that someone was watching her very closely, and from close by. She gazed out the window, *where else could they be watching from?*

Even with all of the sleep she had gotten over the last thirty-six hours, she still felt tired. She put the book in her desk drawer and locked up for the night. Her sleep was heavily interrupted by dreams. She almost felt as if she were really there, just watching the events from outside of her body. The cloaked figures parted and again she saw herself laying on the altar. She awoke with a start. It took her a few minutes to fall back to sleep.

Rolf stood at the fire escape window, quietly waiting for her to find her dream again. Once he was sure that she was out, he silently unlocked the window and stepped inside. He retrieved the book from the desk. Holding the book in his hands, he could easily feel the spirits that dwelled within it—some so old that he couldn't even gauge the level of the Elder that they served. He put everything back in its proper place and made his way out of her room. He went back to the club and William came rushing toward him as soon as he walked in.

"What's wrong?"

"I've been trying to call you. Tasha still isn't here. I've tried texting and calling, and there's been no answer."

"I'll go look for her. Let me know if you hear anything." Rolf broke his own rule and flew over to Tasha's house. He walked around to the back of the house and kicked the door in. The home was dark, but he could tell that there was no sign of a struggle and no sign of Tasha. He wished he had more time to look around, but the sun would be up soon.

At home, his phone rang as he climbed the stairs to his room. The caller ID read *Tasha*. He answered and heard only screaming.

"Don't let them lure you out!" was the last thing he heard before there was complete silence. Then, another woman's voice filled his ears.

"This is only the beginning," she said, then the line went dead. Rolf called Kyle and asked him to go over to Tasha's house. It took Kyle over an hour to get there because the police had completely sealed off the area. He knew one of them from the previous cases at the hospital. He flagged the detective down and asked him what happened.

"First, tell me what you're doing here."

"I know Tasha. We worked together. She didn't show up for her shift last night and wasn't answering her phone, so the boss asked me to swing by and check on her."

"I'm afraid she's been killed."

"What do you mean?"

"It appears that she was burned to death."

"Oh my God…okay. I'll inform the boss. She has no family that we know of, so we will be handling her arrangements." He thanked the officer and returned to the Brownstone. He really wasn't looking forward to sharing this news with Rolf. He and Tasha and shared a long-term relationship. He sat outside until dusk, then went up to see Rolf.

Chapter Eighteen

Christine received a call from the detectives who had been working her cases to find out if she had discovered anything new.

"No, I'm sorry officer. I've been off for the last three days." He told her about the burned body that had been found that morning and asked if she would be willing to help. "Yes, of course." He gave her the address of the residence. Luckily, it would be on her way to work. She called and told the doctor currently on duty that she would be a little late.

Rolf was angry at the way Tasha had been murdered. It was clear now that, whoever was doing this, was doing it because of him. He could think of a single enemy who would carry this much vengeance around with them. He just sat and watched the scene unfolding across the street. It wasn't long before Christine had finished her work at the scene and stepped into the police car to head back to the hospital. Rolf hailed a cab and instructed the driver to take him to Bellevue hospital.

Tristin was waiting for the little rich girl she had turned. When she finally arrived, Tristin slapped her and told her not to ever be late again.

The girl, Sharon, looked like she wanted to strike Tristin right back, until she noticed the look in the other woman's eyes; it was then that she realized she was no longer running the show. At least Sharon was smart enough to lower her eyes and shut her mouth.

"Did anyone see you leave the hospital?" Tristin barked.

"No ma'am."

"Good, come with me."

"Where are we going?" Her question received another sharp slap across the face. By the time they arrived at the Vamp Club, it was standing room only. Tristin looked around for Rolf and was not pleased to discover that he wasn't around. She wanted—no needed—to see his pain after he had treated her like she was just another mistress. She had actually loved him. Tristin stayed at the club for another hour, and even allowed herself to have a glass of the house special. She sent Sharon to the house with clear instructions on how to find her fresh blood. Her thoughts went back to Paris with Rolf. That had been the happiest time of her life. She and Rolf had spent almost a year together as lovers. It had all ended the night he saw her kill a maid that he had been fond of. He left that night and she didn't see him again for decades. They ran into each other again in India. They ended up in bed, but it wasn't the same. He wasn't the same.

He had broken her heart, and because of that, her kills became more and more brutal. One day, she stumbled upon a book of cults and rituals and traced it all the way back to their queen. When Thomas awoke, she would take him to the spot where she knew the queen was being held. The challenge was finding a woman of pure blood to awaken the queen. Tristin had been searching for years, but she felt closer to finding this woman now than she ever had before.

Christine finally made it in to work almost an hour late. She went right in and began her rounds without hesitation. There was still no sign of last night's victim. At the same time, Rolf was making his way up to the isolation ward. He asked the guard to page Christine. After a few moments, she came down and authorized the guard to let him in.

"Let's talk in my office," she said. She led him inside and closed the door behind them. "What can I do for you, Rolf."

"I just wanted to check on the results of the tests that you ordered for Rosha and her family."

"You could have just called."

"But, then I wouldn't be able to see you and ask you out for coffee."

"What makes you think I even like coffee?"

"All doctors drink coffee."

"Is that so?"

"Come on, Doc. What do you say?"

"I guess that would be alright." She told the orderly that she would be back shortly and to call if he needed anything. Rolf and Christine walked in silence until they reached the twenty-four-hour diner a block away from the hospital. Christine ordered coffee and a sandwich for each of the orderlies.

"Aren't you hungry?" she asked when she noticed that Rolf hadn't ordered anything for himself.

"I suffer from a multitude of allergies. It's much easier if I just eat at home."

"I see…" she said looking at him curiously. They made casual conversation and before either of them knew it, a full hour had passed. They walked back to the hospital, discussing books, beliefs, and everything else under the sun. Rolf suddenly stopped in his tracks and looked around.

"Is something the matter?" Christine asked concerned.

"Oh…I, uh…I just had déjà vu. I could almost swear that I've walked with you, just like this, before. It's a strange sensation to have when you've never met the person before," he lied.

Christine knew he wasn't being truthful, but she had dealt with much stranger things over the last couple of weeks.

As soon as Christine was safely inside the hospital, Rolf said, "You might as well come out. What do you want from me Tristin?"

"I want you back."

"I was never yours to begin with. It was just sex Tristin, nothing more."

"Who's the blonde?"

"That's not really any of your business now it is?"

"I suggest you change your tune soon, dear Rolf. You don't want to be on my bad side when Thomas awakens."

"I'll keep that in mind." Tristin huffed and flew away. Rolf decided to hang around for a while, just to make sure that she was really gone. He didn't like putting Christine in Tristin's crosshairs. On his way home, he called Kyle and asked him to put more people at the hospital with Christine.

His house felt so lonely. He missed his talks with Rosha and the way she always tried to take care of him. He remembered the night that she found out about his secret. There was no fear in her eyes, only compassion. He had attended her wedding, been there for her children, comforted her when her husband had been killed by gangsters. But, he had not been there when she needed him most—to save her from a horrific death. Just like he wasn't there for Tasha. He could only imagine what she went through. Even though Tasha didn't always agree with his stance on not hunting, she made it a point to only kill the evil of this world—not innocent mortals. He was going to miss them both very much.

Chapter Nineteen

Christine had always loved watching the sunrise. She wasn't sure why she had agreed to work the night shift. When she arrived at her apartment, her cat met her at the door. It actually wasn't even her cat; the owners just didn't seem to take very good care of it, so she gave it love and food whenever it seemed to need it. She left a plate of tuna out in front of her door and went to run a bubble bath for herself. She lit four candles and climbed into the soothing water. Her mind took her through all of the bizarre events of the last few weeks. Things had been especially weird, even for a psych ward. She was looking forward to going back to the day shift next week. She thought she might still offer to trade for a few night shifts here and there. She kind of liked the lack of hospital politics—besides, she didn't have anyone at home waiting for her like some of the other doctors did. A wave of loneliness suddenly washed over her. As far back as she could remember, it was foster home after foster home. She never had anyone to love her or even care whether or not she died. She suddenly remembered Rolf's soulful eyes. He looked as lonely as she was.

She eventually drained her bath and blew out the candles. She locked up and went to bed. That night, her dreams were of Rolf. He was trying to get to her, but an evil man kept him away. All of a sudden, they both turned into monsters and wolves. They were all around her, and she could do nothing but scream in terror. The scream itself brought her back to consciousness. She could only remember the end of the dream; the rest of it was fuzzy in her memory.

Rolf awoke that evening well rested. He hadn't had any dreams that day. He went about his routine as his mind repeatedly wandered to Christine. He had not been so taken by a woman in a long time—maybe ever. Kyle was at the door, right on time. Rolf smiled a little to himself as he thought, *I could set my watch to this guy.* There was no new news to share, so Kyle just dropped off the new blood supply and told Rolf that he would meet up with him later. Rolf was just about to leave for the club when he heard another knock at the door. It was Victor and his wife.

"This must be serious."

"It is, Rolf."

"Please come in," Rolf said kissing Charlotte's cheek.

"It's been way too long, Rolf. I've missed you my dear boy."

"What has brought you out tonight?"

"It's not good Rolf. Everything we've found so far points to the awakening of Lucia, the queen. The kills you described are exactly as her killings have been recorded throughout history."

"So she is the oldest Elder?"

"Yes, do you suspect that Thomas and Tristin are involved?"

"I hope not, but I wouldn't be surprised if they were. How would they have even found her?"

"We've been looking for thousands of years."

"So what is that going to mean for us?"

"I don't know, Rolf."

"What is it going to take to stop them?"

"They need a virgin with pure blood."

"Well, that will be hard to find in this day and age."

"I certainly hope you are right." Victor put a protective hand on Rolf's shoulder before ushering his wife out of the house. "Take caution, son."

Rolf went down to the club to check in with William. There were a lot of new vampires and their slaves in the club tonight. *No sign of Tristin*, Rolf thought. He almost wished that she was there. Then at least he would be able to keep an eye on her. He suddenly became aware of a young woman staring at him. He could tell she was a new slave. He started to approach, but she bolted out the door. He attempted to follow her, then thought better of it. Instead, he decided to pay a visit to the hospital.

He made it to the entrance of the isolation ward. The guard knew by now to page Dr. Rodgers. It took several moments for her to reach the gate, but when she did, the guard allowed Rolf to enter.

"What can I do for you Rolf?"

"Thought you could use a coffee break." She smiled and went to grab her purse.

Again, she noticed that he didn't order anything. She had a piece of pie with her coffee. It seemed like diners always had the best pie. They talked about nothing in particular, then she asked what he did for a living and why he had such an interest in the bizarre murders that had been happening. Rolf just stared at her for a moment. She didn't think that he was going to answer.

"I own a club downtown. I don't get out much besides being at the club. You already know about Rosha, but my floor manager, Tasha, was also a victim of the murders. Losing two people that I was close to had made this all very personal for me." He noticed a strange look on her face. She said that she had better get back to the hospital. On the way back, they walked in silence. Despite the moment of awkwardness, she seemed to be relaxed. Whether or not she was ready to admit it, she felt comfortable around him. She felt safe with him. They arrived at the entrance to the hospital and he bid her goodnight. He placed a whisper of a kiss on the top of her hand that sent shockwaves through her entire body. He'd lingered a moment as he inhaled the fragrance of her warm blood.

Chapter Twenty

Victor was at the club waiting for Rolf when he returned. Rolf signaled for him to follow him upstairs. They sat in silence for a few minutes until William brought them their drinks. Rolf gave Victor a moment to gather his thoughts.

"What's brought you here Victor?"

"I am afraid that I was right."

"About what exactly?"

"Someone is planning on raising the queen from her tomb."

"How do you know?"

"Thomas will awaken at the blood moon. That gives us ten days to form a plan." Victor said, ignoring Rolf's question. "Have you seen Tristin?"

"Not for the last two nights."

"I was afraid of that."

"Do you think she's the one responsible for uncovering all this?"

"I don't know. She's an Elder, so I can't imagine she would be very happy about having any of her power taken away."

"That's true."

"Well, I had better head home. I just wanted to keep you in the loop. Goodnight Rolf, and happy hunting."

"Same to you. Thanks Victor." Rolf thought back to his talk with Christine. He was going to have to be very careful with her. She was very observant. It was almost time to head home. As he started down the stairs, he saw Christine at the bar.

"I get to see you twice in one night," he said approaching her. "How pleasant."

"I had to come check out this club of yours. I've always been a sucker for vampires," she said laughing at her own joke. William poured Rolf a drink and then fixed Christine another Bloody Mary. He was glad that the club was dark; he was worried that she might notice the difference in their drinks.

"I thought your shift wasn't over until later?"

"It was a really slow night. It's almost like our killer went on holiday."

Over in Eastern Europe, it was just getting dark and Tristin had just woken up. Sharon had already found her a woman to feed on. She wouldn't be allowed to feed until her master's needs had been met first. Tristin hated this part of the world. Some cities still had active vampire hunters. She supposed that that was why Lucia had been brought here. It had taken her over three thousand years to find this spot, and she hoped that it was the right one. She didn't want to deal with the disappointment of another dead end—especially because she knew that Thomas wouldn't tolerate failure at all.

When she arrived at the site where her queen was allegedly buried, several slaves began digging into the side of the mountain. At this rate, it would take several days to make any progress. They were cutting things entirely too close to the deadline. Her thoughts involuntarily turned to Rolf. She missed the man that he was before he began feeling remorse over the mortals. He seemed to have lost his flair. When Thomas awakened, Rolf would have to come back into the coven or risk ending up like Tasha. She supervised the slaves for another few minutes before heading back to the castle.

Rolf insisted on walking Christine home from the club. When he left her safely in the care of her doorman, he returned home himself. *Well, that went well*, he thought. *Maybe, I'll actually be able to tell her that I'm a vampire…someday.* Christine locked her apartment door behind her and sat down with her book and a glass of wine. She had been intrigued by the club. There was an obvious undertone of evil, but she felt protected by Rolf.

When Rolf returned home, he could tell that Kyle had already come and gone. He called him and asked him to come back to the Brownstone. They were really going to have to step up their search before the Blood Moon came into orbit. The watchers would be a great help, and Victor could contribute some sources also. Rolf reflected on all of the changes that had taken place over the last two hundred years—most of it for the better. But, he knew that would all change once Thomas was back. He thought of Christine. He had never felt such a draw to a mortal woman before. This was not the time for him to be having feelings like this. He needed to stay away from her if he wanted to keep her safe.

"I've tried to locate Tristin, but haven't had any luck." Rolf paced the floor, "I'm pretty sure she's gone after the queen. Kyle, I need you to go to the doctor's home and retrieve the book that is in the left side drawer of her desk. Make sure you are not seen.

"Do you want me to make it look like a break-in?"

"Yes. Get the book back and lock it in with the blood." Rolf decided to go see Victor while Kyle was seeing to his task. He wanted to let Victor know what his plan was and to inform him about the book.

"Why hadn't you said anything about this before?" Victor asked.

"I wasn't sure that the book had anything to do with this, but now I am sure that it does."

"Who is this woman, Rolf?"

"She's a doctor at Bellevue Hospital. She has been handling all of the rogue vampire bite victims.

"I see. I haven't seen you like this in a long time," Victor told him.

"I can't help the way I feel."

"Just tread lightly my friend. I don't want to see this destroy you. Bring the book to me as soon as you have it."

"Of course, Victor." As he walked away, Rolf couldn't help but feel like Victor was acting very strangely. He would have liked to stop by the hospital, but he was running out of time. He felt very restless, like he was on the verge of a major breakthrough. When he arrived home, Kyle was waiting for him with the book in hand.

"Did anyone see you?"

"No, of course not."

"Okay, let's get this thing copied, and then we can return it." Once that was done, Kyle took it back to Christine's apartment. Rolf poured himself a night cap, shut all the curtains, and sat down to read. After two hours, he called it a morning and went upstairs to sleep.

Chapter Twenty-One

Tristin was livid. They were running out of time. If she disappointed Thomas, she would lose her position as an Elder, and she loved the power too much to allow that to happen. Even if she had to share the power with Lucia, she would still be one of the most powerful vampires in the coven. If only she could convince Rolf to stand by her side. But, he was so set on his course to save the humans, that he had lost sight of who and what he was. She was determined to remind him.

Just then, Sharon entered the room, telling Tristin that one of the men from the dig was here to speak with her. She dismissed Sharon and made her way slowly down the staircase. She hoped that her eagerness for good news didn't show. She was informed that someone had knocked over one of the pillars, collapsing the entrance. She knew that this was the sign of some force working against her. She shrieked at the top of her lungs in anger and immediately killed the man who had brought such terrible news.

She went over to the dig sight and the foreman told her that they were making good time, even with the setbacks. There were still several hours until dawn. Tristin warned him that there would be severe punishment for all involved if they were not finished in time. The foreman and his men did not question her threat at all. They could see that her evil far outweighed her beauty. Tristin loved the fact that she scared people. She loved the feeling of power it gave her.

Christine was on her way to the diner; she just had to get out of the hospital for a little while. She had a new patient—a sixteen-year-old girl with bi-polar disorder who was off of her medications. Her heart ached for this girl. She had been in and out of hospitals since she was ten, with no known relatives. This girl needed help—needed someone to care. She was so immersed in reading her new patient's file, that Christine didn't notice the elderly man approaching her. Victor wanted to see this woman for himself; he wanted to make sure that Rolf wasn't going to end up hurt again. He just stood watching her for a moment. She was completely oblivious to his presence. Victor, on the other hand, could easily feel the passion she felt for whatever she was doing. One of the files fell from the table and onto the floor. Victor bent to pick it up and handed it to her. He could see the sadness and pain in her eyes as she took the file from him. She thanked him, but he just smiled and walked away.

Christin brought herself back to the present moment and found herself wondering where Rolf had been. She hadn't seen him for a few days—or, nights, rather. She drank the rest of her coffee, paid her check, and then started back to the hospital. She went straight to her new patient's room. Christine was relieved to see her resting peacefully. She hoped that she would be feeling a little better when she awoke. There was no way to know how long she had been off of her meds, but Christine was looking forward to being able to speak with her. She finished the rest of her rounds and went back to her office to complete some reports.

At around three o'clock that morning, the guard called to let her know that she had a visitor. She was expecting Rolf, but instead, she was greeted by a young man who had the kindest eyes she had ever seen. He introduced himself as Kyle Winters. He said he worked in the lab at St. Marks.

"I've been sent to bring you over the lab results from the first pile of ashes you had tested."

"Thank you very much." She said taking the reports back to her office. She was disappointed to see that there wasn't really anything special revealed in them. The sun was up by the time her shift came to a close, so she decided to walk home. It was a beautiful morning. She was only about a block away from her building when she suddenly got the sense that she was being watched again; this was the first time that it had happened during the day. She went straight upstairs, and as soon as she opened her door, gasped at the mess inside. Her entire place had been trashed again. She searched through the mess and found that several things were missing. She called down to security and then notified the police. The security tapes had been erased. All that she could do was try to put her home back in order and request that her super change the locks…again.

Chapter Twenty-Two

Rolf awoke with a feeling of urgency. He knew he needed to make some headway or life for all would change very soon. Kyle arrived and he told Rolf about his meeting with Dr. Rodgers.

"You changed the reports?"

"Yes, and it went smoothly," Kyle assured him.

"Well done."

"She seems nice."

"Yes, she is."

"Oh, before I forget, an orderly told me about a new patient—a sixteen-year-old girl named Leah. It was just strange because no one knows where she came from. Her entire life has been in and out of hospitals. No bite marks or anything, but maybe she is the one that everyone is looking for."

"I'll head over to the hospital. I've been trying to stay away, but this is important. I don't know how she's involved in all of this, but I'm sure that she is."

"It sure looks that way. I'll see you later Rolf."

"Thanks for everything my friend."

Christine was in a meeting with her supervisor. He was requesting that she change shifts with one of the other doctors. She, of course, agreed. Before she left, she made her way to the young girl's room. The orderly told her that the patient seemed to be having a peaceful day.

"That's good news."

"A man came by asking about her, but I told him that visitors weren't allowed on this floor."

"Did he leave a name?"

"No, ma'am, but he did look kind of familiar."

"Okay, thank you. Let me know if he comes back please."

"Of course."

About an hour later, the guard called her to the gate. It was Rolf. She smiled as she approached.

"Would you like to join me for some coffee?"

"You are just in time; I was just about to take my break." She left instructions with the orderly and they left the hospital. "I've missed seeing you the last couple of nights," she admitted.

"The club has been so busy lately. But, you have certainly been on my mind a lot."

"Well, I guess that counts for something," she said smiling. "Hey, you weren't at the hospital earlier by any chance, were you?"

"Guilty as charged."

"May I ask why you were asking about my new patient?"

"I was just curious if she was another bite victim."

"Nope, just a very sick and lost young lady."

"Well, I'm sure she's getting the care that she needs now that she has you to look after her."

"Thank you for saying that, Rolf. Sometimes I feel like I'm fighting a losing battle."

"I can understand that, but at least you care." They ordered some coffee. She turned down the pie this time.

"So, your club has been extra busy?"

"Yes, it always is when the full moon comes around. But now, there is a special moon coming. Did you know that we haven't had a Blood Moon since 1982?"

"I didn't know that. Interesting." They just sat there smiling at each other for a moment. Then, she looked down at her watch. "I better be getting back."

"Of course." They walked back in silence. "Well, here we are. I hope the rest of your night is calm."

"Thanks Rolf, you too."

Chapter Twenty-Three

Tristin was headed over to the dig site. They had made acceptable progress over the last seventy-two hours. She was hopeful that they would find the queen soon. She was pleased that they had discovered a new tunnel. Tristin entered and marveled over the markings on the wall. She was sure they dated back thousands of years. Tristin was beginning to get a very good feeling about this mission. She was more than ready to see this business over with.

There weren't any more discoveries that night, but they all felt that they were getting close to something big. Tristin looked around for Sharon, but she was nowhere to be found. *What a pain in the ass this woman is*, she thought angrily. She would get rid of her as soon as they got back to New York. The locals were already starting to complain about missing town-folk. She was almost tempted to follow Rolf's lead and go to the blood bank. It was only an hour or so before sunrise, so she decided to go back to the castle.

She found Sharon with one of the servants, talking quietly in the corner of the kitchen. Her flawless hearing allowed her to pick up every word, despite how far away she was. The servant was telling Sharon that he would help her get away. Tristin hadn't planned on killing anyone else while she was here, but there was no way that she could let this go unpunished.

Sharon looked up, saw the look on her master's face, and visibly went white. Tristin instructed her to go up to their suite and not to come back down. Sharon knew that this didn't mean anything good for her new friend, but, *better him than me.* Tristin led the servant down to the dungeon. As soon as they arrived in the chamber, she killed him, drained his blood, and left him on the floor for the rats. She went back upstairs and slapped Sharon so hard that it knocked her to the floor.

"If I ever have to do this again, you won't like what happens next," Tristin growled through gritted teeth. Sharon cringed as Tristin left the room, slamming the door behind her. Sharon knew that her master would sleep for hours, which was a great relief. She looked all over the castle but couldn't find any sign of her friend. Giving up her search, she retired to her own room, and fell into a deep sleep.

Back in New York, Rolf was having a very bad day. He couldn't sleep because he kept having terrible dreams about Christine and her new patient, Leah. He finally gave up on trying to sleep and went downstairs to pour himself a double. By the time Kyle arrived, he was pacing back and forth through the living room.

"What's going on, Rolf?"

"I'm not entirely sure. I just have this feeling of doom, and I can't shake it. I can't sleep because I have these awful dreams about Christine. And now, I'm dreaming about that young girl in the hospital. I've never even seen her, but she's been in every dream. I just feel like there is nothing we can do to stop Thomas."

"We'll figure it out, Rolf. You'll see."

"I hope so, because if we don't, there will be so much blood shed. I'm going to see Victor, then I'll be at the club if you need me. I feel like I've been neglecting it and it's our busiest time of the year right now. Did you put extra people at the hospital?"

"Yes."

"Good. Get some rest if you can. I'll see you later." Rolf bid him farewell and traveled the short distance to Victor's house. Charlotte answered the door on the second knock.

"It's so good to see you my dear. Unfortunately, Victor is not here. He got called away, something to do with Thomas I believe."

"Oh. Well please just let him know that I came by."

"Of course, dear."

Christine was busy from the moment from she arrived at the hospital that evening. She hadn't even had a chance to check on Leah yet. She hoped that things would slow down soon. She wasn't sure why she was drawn to this girl; she just seemed so lost and alone. She saw much of herself in her.

The evening hadn't calmed down at all, but she managed to sneak to the diner for a cup of coffee. She thought about the last time she was here with Rolf. Almost as if her thoughts had summoned him, Rolf came walking through the door of the diner precisely at that moment.

"How are you?" he asked.

"Exhausted. We've been so busy tonight."

"How's Leah?"

"She's still not very alert, but that's not unusual with the amount of sedative we're administering.

"I'm sorry, I know we technically aren't supposed to be talking about your patients."

"It's okay." The walk back to the hospital was quiet. She was actually enjoying not having anything to say. They arrived and Rolf bid her goodnight.

Chapter Twenty-Four

At the dig site, Tristin was happy to finally get news that they had found something positive. She was ready to get out of this god-forsaken town. She was getting really tired of the police questioning her about her missing servants. She had become carless and she knew it.

"My lady, we've broken through to an inner chamber. The markings inside are very old." The foreman informed her. Tristin went to see for herself. She was pleased. This was her most promising dig yet. Tristin noticed that Sharon still hadn't showed up yet. This was getting to be a bigger problem than it was worth. The woman's only job was to bring her people who wouldn't be missed. She had been good at it so far because Tristin would drink from her if she couldn't manage the task. The foreman helped her out of the tunnel, and she headed back to the castle in search of her worthless servant.

"I've found one. He's in the dungeon waiting for you," Sharon said, meeting Tristin in the foyer. Tristin didn't even acknowledge her as she went straight to the stairwell. She was famished. The man looked tattered and unhealthy. Again, she longed to be back in the states where even the homeless took better care of themselves. She drained him and left his body in a heap on the floor. His would be the ninth body disposed of here.

Tristin went to her room and closed herself in her coffin. They would have to keep the queen's coffin locked until the Blood Moon. That was when they would conduct the ceremony to bring her back to life, with Thomas awakening at her side. Everything needed to be in order, otherwise it would be two hundred years before they got another chance.

Rolf sat in his office at the club, concerned that he hadn't heard from Victor yet. It wasn't like him to miss an appointment. He waited a little while longer, then decided to head home. Once he arrived, he noticed that Kyle had already stopped by. Rolf hoped that he was being cautious. He couldn't stand to lose someone else that he cared about. He had started up the stairs to his room when the phone rang. It was Victor asking if they could meet at dusk. Rolf didn't want to wait, but the sun was already beginning to rise. He agreed and tried his best to get a good day's rest.

Christine went home two hours after her shift ended. She was sitting with Leah, hoping to make some progress with her. Just went she thought she was getting somewhere, the young girl just completely shut down. After getting home, Christine poured herself a drink and grabbed her book. She thumbed through to the last chapter. The photos astounded her. They were images from her dream. The only difference was that it wasn't her laying on the altar; it was Leah. There was no logical explanation for what she was seeing on the pages of this old book. She thought about showing it to Rolf and seeing what he made of all this.

Chapter Twenty-Five

Tristin arrived at the dig site. No new graphics had been found, but she just knew deep in her bones that this was the right location. She was still having trouble with Sharon. She wouldn't be surprised if she ended up killing the damn girl before they even made it back to New York. When she thought of New York, she thought of Rolf. She would either win him back or kill him; there was no other alternative.

She noticed there was a lot of energy from the crew on the site this evening. She noticed a young man standing at the entrance to the cave. She hadn't seen him before. She called Sharon over and told her to find out what she could about him.

Christine arrived early so she could spend some extra time with Leah. She brought the book of rituals with her. She requested that the security guard let her know as soon as Rolf arrived—if he arrived. Leah was awake when Christine walked in, and still very agitated. Christine really didn't want to put her on any more medications, but she knew that she would need to at least get some Ativan and Benadryl—hopefully that would help calm her. Christine sat with Leah until she fell asleep. She looked so young and innocent. Christine wondered how such a girl could end up so sick and passed around from treatment center to treatment center. After she left Leah's side, she clocked in and began her usual rounds. There still had not been a single vampire attack or mysteriously missing body. Christine laughed that things had actually become fairly boring since all of the strange excitement had ended.

Rolf awoke at dusk and made his way downstairs. He was eager to get to Victor's. When he arrived, Victor was already waiting at the door. He led Rolf into his study. As soon as the door was closed behind them, Victor said, "Its worse than I thought, Rolf. Has there been any sign of Tristin yet?"

"No, I have several people keeping a lookout for her, but nothing has been reported."

"I've found a scholar who has helped us analyze the book of rituals. They are looking for the queen. It looks like they are planning to recreate the sacred ritual on the Blood Moon to awaken her and Thomas together. They are in need of a human sacrifice—an innocent. We have to stop this. From what I have read, this Lucia, the queen, makes Thomas and Tristin look like saints. I think the way that Rosha and Tasha were murdered was done as a tribute to Lucia, by Tristin."

"I can't believe how evil she has become..."

"Rolf, she's always been this way. You were just too taken by her beauty to see it."

"I know you are right, Victor. I guess I just still wanted to believe that she could never be capable of something like this."

"Giving people, and vampires, the benefit of the doubt will be your greatest downfall my friend."

"I have to agree with my husband on this, Rolf," Charlotte slipped quietly into the study "I'm so sorry to just barge in like this, but I thought you might appreciate another's perspective—especially since we are dealing with two women here. And I just so happen to be a woman." Rolf received his usual kiss on the cheek. He couldn't remember what it felt like to have parents, but he imagined that Victor and his wife were as close as he would get to having any. They had always been there for him— even when he thought he didn't need anyone. After he left them, he made his way to the hospital. Rolf couldn't help but look forward to seeing Christine. He couldn't believe how comfortable he was becoming with having her in his life. In certain ways, she reminded him a lot of his wife, but much stronger.

He arrived at the gate and the security guard informed him that Christine was already expecting him. He thought nervously that perhaps he was becoming way too familiar around here. The guard escorted him up to the isolation ward where

Christine was waiting for him. She led him to her office and offered him a cup of coffee. She told him about the book, her dreams, and about the strange experience she'd had at the non-existent bookstore. She showed him the photo in the last ritual.

"I'm not sure what I'm looking at here," he said.

"Follow me," she instructed, leading him down the hall. Christine unlocked the door to Leah's room and brought him inside. As soon as his eyes fell on the young woman in the bed, he was dumbfounded. It was the girl from his dreams—the girl from the photo he had just looked at in a book that was thousands of years old. He tried not to let his face give away his surprise, but Christine had already noticed his reaction. "You see it don't you?"

"I do."

"How is this possible?"

"Have you shown anyone else?"

"No."

"Let's head to the diner, so we can talk freely about this," Rolf suggested. Christine agreed and grabbed her purse from her office.

They sat at the table in silence for a moment before Christine finally spoke.

"What do you think it all means, Rolf?"

"What makes you think that I know?" She was a little taken aback by his tone.

"I…I don't know. I guess because you started showing up at the hospital when all of this strangeness began."

"Doctor, I don't know much more than you do, I assure you. But, I'm trying desperately to get to the bottom of it. I've already lost too many people that were very close to me. People that I loved, and I want to make sure that I don't lose any more." There was silence between them again. "We had better get you back. I should really check on things at the club."

"Of course," she almost whispered. Once she was back at the hospital and Rolf had left for the club, Christine returned to Leah's room. She walked in as the girl was in the middle of a vicious nightmare. Christine couldn't wake her, so she just sat holding her hand and trying to soothe her. She waited until Leah seemed to have found a peaceful rest again, then left for home.

As Rolf neared the club, his mind worried tremendously about the role that Christine would play in all of this when it finally came to a head. In spite of the fact that she was a mortal, and there could never really be anything between them, he found himself falling a little more in love with her every day.

Chapter Twenty-Six

Rolf awoke the next morning to a pounding at his door. He looked around and realized that it was already several hours after dusk. He opened the door to find a very anxious Victor.

"Victor, what is it?"

"We were supposed to meet at dusk. I was very worried."

"My apologies. I can't imagine how I managed to oversleep so long. Please come in, I have some information to share." They entered the dining room and Rolf brought in a chilled bottle. "The young girl in the ritual photo, she is lying in a hospital bed at Bellevue as we speak. She is in the care of Dr. Rodgers."

"My, this just gets more intriguing with each passing day."

"What do you think it all means? And what does it have to do with Tristin?"

"I believe that she is just a pawn that Thomas is using to carry out his plan while he is at rest. I have noticed several new vampires in town. They are starting to gather Rolf. We need to get on top of this soon."

Tristin heard a loud commotion as she descended the stairs into the entry hall.

"What the hell is going on?" she shouted at Sharon.

"It seems the men have managed to break into the chamber. They have located a casket made of iron. It has chains all around it. Apparently, one man tried to open it and fell down dead in an instant."

"I gave orders that it not be opened. No one else is to go down there, do you understand?"

"Yes ma'am."

Tristin felt as if she were on top of the world as she walked onto the dig site. The thing she had been searching for hundreds of years was finally within her grasp. She entered the chamber and poured a vile of blood over the casket. Legend had it that doing this would prevent the evil from killing. She thought about all the wasted blood from the worker who had tried to open the coffin. She had been so good lately. She knew that Rolf would have been impressed with her.

She returned to the surface and instructed the men to load the casket onto a truck and ordered Sharon to have the pilot standing by. There were only seven workers left and Tristin happily killed all of them once the casket had been securely loaded. She piled their bodies into the tunnel and collapsed the entrance. Once the plane was ready, she had the servants bring her things out and she boarded the plane. Sharon could hardly sit still; she was so excited to be finally going home. She missed her social life more than anything else. She knew she would never get that back as long as she was forced to serve Tristin. She wished that Tristin would just turn her completely so that she could at least be out of this weird limbo state. She had done so many bad things in her life; she knew she was being punished for all of them.

Christine woke up feeling as though she were sitting on a ledge with no way to get off. She forced herself to eat a bit, then got ready for her shift. When she arrived in the isolation ward, the day shift doctor informed her about how agitated Leah had become. She had to be restrained and sedated. Christine thanked him for the update and went straight to Leah's room. She was asleep, so Christine left her alone. Leah was still knocked out by the time Christine clocked out for the evening. *That must have been some sedative*, Christine thought as she wrote up medication orders for the day shift. She made a mental note to arrive a little earlier the next evening.

Rolf had planned on going to see Christine, but the club was slammed, and he just couldn't find the time to get away. New vampires from several covens were continuing to flock to the city. There was still no sign of Tristin from what he understood. When he arrived at the Brownstone just before dawn, Kyle was waiting for him.

"We are still watching the airports and train stations, but so far there is nothing to report. There has been lots of chatter about the 'big day'. They are saying that it is going to be a great day for loyal vampires and a tragic day for mortals."

"Yes, I have heard that too. Victor says the same. I hate all of this waiting around, but there isn't much more we can do at this point. Get some rest my friend. I will see you tonight."

"Take care of yourself, Rolf. You need your rest too."

"Have I ever told you how much I appreciate you? Thank you for being someone that I can count on. Your help has been invaluable."

"I'm here for you buddy. It's going to be okay."

"I know." Rolf shook his friend's hand and went upstairs to his room. He tried his best to rejuvenate. He knew that he would need to be at his best when this all finally played out.

Chapter Twenty-Seven

Tristin was glad to be back in New York City. It was still several days before the Blood Moon, and to celebrate her glorious find, she went to the Vamp Club. It was nearly standing room only where she arrived, but she could tell that Rolf wasn't around. She pushed her way to the bar and asked William where he was.

"I don't know. I haven't seen him yet tonight, but when I do I will tell him that you are looking for him."

"I'm sure you will. Get me a drink and a table in the back."

"Yes ma'am."

Kyle missed Rolf at the Brownstone, so he figured he could find him at the club. As soon as he walked in, he noticed Tristin at the bar. William subtly motioned for Kyle to leave. The hospital was the next likely place to find Rolf. As he approached the hospital, he noticed Rolf and Christine on their way to the diner. Rolf saw Kyle coming down the sidewalk and motioned for him to wait where he was until they got back.

Christine could sense that Rolf had a lot on his mind. He was quieter than usual tonight. He was torn between wanting to feel at peace in her presence, to know that all of this would soon change, and they would be lucky to make it out with their lives. Then, he realized that, with everything that had been going on, he and Kyle hadn't made any progress on the formula that would hopefully make him a day-walker. *My how priorities change*, Rolf thought with a saddened smirk.

"Has there been any progress in the young woman's case?" he asked Christine, breaking his train of runaway thoughts.

"Not really. Nothing other than the fact that she seems much more agitated lately. There have been several nights where we have needed to restrain her just to keep her from hurting herself." They finished their coffee, and Rolf held the door for her as they began the walk back to the hospital. Around the corner from the hospital, he wished her a goodnight and turned to leave. She found it strange because, normally, he would walk her all the way to the isolation ward's gate. She shrugged it off and proceeded with her rounds for the night—purposely leaving Leah as her last patient. She was happy to see Leah awake, until she noticed how aggravated she was becoming—and fast.

"They're coming after me. They will kill me. They are going to kill me." Leah screamed. She was quickly put back under sedation and Christine took notes on everything that came out of her mouth.

Christine straightened her office and headed for home. It was a dark morning; she thought it looked like rain. She hoped so; she always slept better when it was raining. Instead of going straight home, she stopped at the diner for breakfast. A man dressed in all black came in and sat at the table behind her. He seemed familiar to her, but she couldn't quite place how she knew him.

Kyle noticed that she had changed her routine so he followed her into the diner, hoping that she wouldn't remember him. There were only nine other people in the place, staff included.

Chapter Twenty-Eight

Rolf had received a message from Victor saying that Tristin was back. She had flown in and requested that a large pick-up truck be available for her. That meant that she had found the queen.

"So, it begins, Rolf. Tread softly my boy." Rolf heard a knock at the door and wasn't surprised to see Kyle.

"Doctor Rodgers changed her routine tonight."

"Oh? How so?"

"She stopped at the diner to have breakfast before she went home."

"By herself?"

"Yes."

"Hmmm, anything else odd about her behavior?"

"Not really. Besides the fact that she is still glued to that book of hers."

"Okay, thank you for the update my friend. Good day."

"Rest well, Rolf."

Across town, Christine was making her way upstairs to her apartment. She had really enjoyed her breakfast. Normally, she wouldn't feel comfortable going to a restaurant alone, but lately it just didn't seem to bother her. She felt safe.

Later that afternoon, the sound of the phone ringing woke Christine from her sleep. It was the hospital. Leah was becoming violent and trying to break out of her restraints. Christine told them that she would be there as soon as she could and instructed that they not leave her alone, even for a second. She arrived at the hospital thirty minutes later. The orderly met her at the gate.

"How is she?"

"Getting worse by the second."

"What have you given her?" She filled her in on all of the mediations and the dosages as they hurried to her room. After reviewing the chart briefly, Christine order a new drug cocktail that calmed Leah almost immediately. Christine was able to safely check her vitals and told the orderly that she wanted constant surveillance on this room. She stopped to check in on Leah several times throughout the night.

Around three o'clock in the morning security paged Christine letting her know that she had a visitor. She rushed down expecting to see Rolf, but instead, she came face to face with an older, regal looking woman she had never met before.

"You look like you were expecting someone else, Dr. Rodgers," the woman said with a smirk.

"I'm sorry, do we know each other?"

"We have a mutual friend."

"I think you may be mistaken. I only know people from work."

"Rolf is like a son to me. You have no idea what he has been through and I will not allow him to feel hurt like that again."

"Ma'am, with all due respect, I have only met with Rolf for coffee a few times. I'm really not sure what you're talking about. I have no intention of hurting anyone."

"Just remember that in the days to come. Here is my number doctor. When you need to call, I will help you stay alive. Goodnight Dr. Rodgers."

Christine was still puzzling over the conversation when Rolf walked up.

"I just had the strangest conversation," she told him. "This woman said that she thinks of you like a son, and that I can call her when I need help to stay alive. Didn't you run into her in the hallway?"

"No, but I have a feeling I know who it was. Don't pay her any mind. She is protective, that's all. Anyway, how is your night going otherwise?"

"Oh fine. I was called in early to deal with Leah. She was very agitated and was saying the strangest things, but she's resting peacefully now."

"Have you had any more dreams about the book?"

"Yes, and they are getting more vivid every time I have them."

"How so?"

"The faces. They become clearer, and I can physically feel the evil in the room. What do you think it means?"

"I'm not sure, but I hope you know you can call me if you ever need something."

"Hmm, that's the second time tonight I've gotten that offer."

"It is meant most sincerely."

"Thank you, Rolf." He smiled at her. "Would you like to see Leah before you go?"

"Yes, of course." They both just stood there staring at the young woman for a moment. "She seems too young to be in this much emotional turmoil."

"I agree. I can hardly allow her to be conscious without her trying to hurt herself and escape. I've ordered someone to stay with her around the clock.

"That's probably for the best. Well, I really should get going. I have taken too much of your time tonight."

"Goodnight Rolf."

As soon as Rolf stepped out onto the sidewalk, he immediately felt a presence. Although it was far from Tristin's evil presence, he had felt it following him all night.

"Alright come out. Show yourself." he ordered.

"Relax, Rolf. It's just me."

"Colin? What are you doing here?" Rolf asked his brother.

"You didn't think that I was going to miss Thomas' awakening, did you?"

"Of course not."

"You know once it happens, you're going to have a choice to make, right?"

"Yes, I know," Rolf answered, pinching the bridge of his nose.

"And, the two of you didn't exactly end on a good note."

"No, we didn't. And you made sure that you were the golden child."

"Who's the blonde?"

"A doctor I met when my housekeeper was murdered."

"Rolf, you really need to stop getting so involved with the humans. It has never ended well for you."

"You would know, Colin."

"I was only looking out for you, brother."

"I don't need anyone looking out for me."

"What happened to you Rolf? We used to be so close."

"That was six hundred years ago."

"Yeah well, maybe I still miss it." Rolf just stared at his brother without response. "I wish you good luck, Rolf." Colin turned and disappeared into the night.

Chapter Twenty-Nine

As soon as Christine left the hospital she knew she was being watched. Kyle's man was waiting for her with clear instructions not to let her out of his sight. There seemed to be a new current of energy going through the city—an evil one. It pulsed and only grew stronger with each passing hour. If Tristin was able to pull this whole thing off with the queen and Thomas, it would mean utter chaos and destruction for the human race. It could in fact bring about slavery for all mankind.

Tristin was pacing the floor, awaiting dusk. She could feel the excitement racing through her body. She hadn't felt this alive in hundreds of years. Tomorrow night would initiate seven nights of rituals leading up to the Blood Moon and the great awakening. Finally, vampires would rule the world as intended. Sharon shivered as she heard Tristin's sinister laugh echo through the house. She knew that she would never escape the madness; in fact, she had an awful feeling that the madness had only begun.

That afternoon, Christine's phone started ringing hours before her alarm was due to go off.

"Hello," she answered with sleep still in her voice.

"Dr. Rodgers, someone tried to break into Leah's room. He had stolen an ID from another staff member. He was attempting to loosen her restraints when we caught him."

"I'll be right over. Don't you dare leave her alone again." Christine arrived to total chaos in the isolation ward. "What's going on?" she yelled to anyone who would answer. The kidnapper was in a hospital bed as a team tried to resuscitate him.

"He just collapsed." the guard told her. Upon closer inspection, she could see the small puncture wounds in his neck. *Oh God, it's happening again*, she thought putting a hand over her mouth.

"Dr. Rodgers, have you been watching the news?"

"No, why?"

"There was a string of brutal murders last night in an old warehouse—very similar to the ones that you dealt with."

"What morgue are they in?"

"St. Marks."

Rolf, and others in support of their cause, met at Victor's.

"Victor, we've been able to translate more of the book you submitted. It seems as though Thomas and Lucia are planning to become one in their power. They will merge to become the most vicious of our kind. They want to use this power to take us back into the Dark Ages. No one will doubt our existence. There will no longer be any balance between our race and the humans."

"Work faster. There must be something in the book that will tell us how they can be stopped."

"In the meantime, I am going to the hospital to check on the girl," Rolf told them.

Rolf arrived at the hospital and requested Dr. Rodgers as he always did. He tried to wait patiently for her to come down, but as fifteen minutes turned into thirty, he grew anxious. She was finally able to make it down to greet him; the wave of warmth and relief that rushed through his body shocked him. The security guard smiled to himself as he watched the subtle smile play across the doctor's lips. He could count on one hand how many times he'd seen her smile over the years. The smile was unfamiliar, but very welcomed.

"How is everything here?" Rolf asked her. "Is Leah coming around?"

"She's not doing well at all actually. We need to keep her sedated around the clock and every time she seems to need a higher dose," she answered, leading him to her office. She closed the door behind him and noticed that he looked especially serious tonight. "Rolf, what is it?"

"I'm not sure how to say what I need to say to you…I know you can feel a change in the city; I can see it in your face."

"Yes, it feels…undeniably evil."

"It is. I don't want to frighten you, but we are quickly running out of time."

"What are you talking about?"

"The dreams you've been having are about to happen for real. Some of the rogue vampires in the city have banded together to raise an evil queen from thousands of years ago. Carrying out the rituals in your book is going to help them do that. But I…I'm one of the good guys, and I'm going to do everything in my power not to let that happen. Because if it does, well…it will mean slaughter for the human race and enslavement for the lucky few that survive." Christine had turned away from him to look out the small window in the office. There was only silence between them. "Oh, for goodness's sake Christine, please say something." She turned back around to face him.

"So, you really do exist? Vampires I mean."

"Yes, I know this is a lot to take in, but please trust me. I really am one of the good guys."

"I'm not afraid of you Rolf. I've always believed. Ever since I was a little girl; I just always thought that I was weird or crazy."

"You're not crazy. This is all very real. There is an Elder who is about to awaken named Thomas. He is going to awaken together with the queen. I need you to come to this address as soon as your shift is over. Please try not to worry; I will do everything I possibly can to ensure that you are protected."

"I really am in danger?"

"I'm afraid so."

"Why? What do I have to do with any of this?"

"I'm not sure yet, but I think your dreams are a big piece of the puzzle."

"Okay, I will meet with you after my shift. I will bring the book with me as well. There was a letter hidden away on the inside cover. It's in the same language that the final ritual is written in."

"Be careful Christine, please." He gently kissed her cheek then left the hospital. When he was outside, he noticed Colin waiting for him. "Are you following me?"

"Of course not. I was actually here to check on a patient."

"What patient could you possibly know in this hospital?"

"Why don't you tell me why you're here first, and then maybe I'll tell you why I'm here."

"Go to hell Colin and stay out of my way." Colin just laughed and walked away.

"She's looking for you Rolf," Colin called over his shoulder. As Rolf walked to the club, he was saddened by the amount of darkness in the world. He had managed to surround himself with a little bit of light—Rosha, Kyle, and now Christine—people who were willing to befriend the monster in him. Arriving at the club, he immediately noticed that they were at capacity. There was a line out the door and around the corner. He made his way to the bar and signaled for William to bring him a drink.

Just as he lifted the glass to his lips, Tristin sat down beside him.

"I've missed you Rolf, how are you?"

"Really? Can't say that I've even thought about you. Were you away?"

"Now, now, Rolf. That's not very nice. You know I still love you."

"Enough to stop whatever it is you are up to?"

"I would if I could. Unfortunately, it is out of my hands at this point, my love. This is our destiny. Come with us. Stand with us. Stand beside me, and we will rule together.

"Do you really think that Thomas is going to give you anything even close to the power that you are imagining? If so, then you are an even bigger fool than I gave you credit for."

"You will soon regret those words, Rolf." She threw her drink in his face and walked away. *She's probably right*, he thought to himself as he watched her leave. *It wasn't wise to make her so angry.* He couldn't help himself; just having her near him made his skin crawl. Victor took her seat a moment later and scolded him for the way he had treated Tristin.

"I know, I know. She just brings out the worst in me. I can't help it. Any luck with the book?"

"It's coming along slowly, but we're not giving up."

"Good. Well I have someone with eyes on Tristin and Colin."

"Very good. Get some rest my boy. We will need every bit of strength in the coming days."

Chapter Thirty

Kyle made his way over to Rolf's. He repeatedly looked over his shoulder. He was used to doing the watching; being watched was a feeling that made him tremendously uneasy. Rolf wasn't back yet, so he was just going to let himself in. As he put the key in the lock, Tristin grabbed him from behind and tore open his throat. After feeding on him, she left his lifeless body on the front porch for Rolf to find when he got home. Colin waited for her at the bottom step. They left just moments before Rolf made it home.

He ran up the steps and held Kyle in his arms sobbing. When he was able to regain his composure, he looked around to make sure that no one was around, then brought Kyle's body inside. Despite the pain he felt with the other deaths, this loss was devastating. Rolf closed all of the curtains and placed a call to the hospital. Christine answered and could immediately hear the anguish in his voice.

"Tell me where you are. I'll be there soon, she said before he could even tell her what had happened. He gave her his address and sat down to drink. He wished he could drink whiskey again or take a magic pill that would make him forget everything. *See, this is why you don't let people in, especially mortals...because they die,* he scolded himself. And now, he was putting perhaps the most important mortal into the line of fire. He sat, thinking about the first time he met Kyle. He had been attempting to rob the blood bank, and Kyle caught him. Kyle had taken notice of the missing blood and hid, waiting to catch the thief.

"Look, don't kill me," Kyle had said. "I want to help you."

"And just how do you think that you can help me?"

"I'm going to school to become a hematologist, but I want to specialize in blood abnormalities. Maybe we can help each other. I can help you be normal, or at least make it so that you can walk in the light, and you just have to let me study you."

"Do you really think it's possible?"

"Yes, of course. Vampires are real, so I guess that means anything is possible. Plus, you won't have to steal blood anymore." Rolf's thoughts of Kyle were interrupted when he heard Christine come in. She asked to see Kyle's body.

"My God, this is so much worse than the others."

"Yes, the vampire responsible, her name is Tristin. She's vicious and merciless, and I'm afraid that it's only getting worse."

"I don't know, Rolf; this seems really personal."

"It is. We used to be lovers before I met my wife."

"Oh…I see. How long have you been alone, Rolf?"

"About a hundred and fifty years."

"And she's still after you?"

"She's very stubborn."

"Clearly.

"Look, I asked you to be here because I can't leave the house until dusk. I need you to go to this address and tell them that Kyle sent you. Then, I need you to send them here."

"Okay. And here, here's the letter I was telling you about."

"Thank you, Christine."

"I'll see you tonight. And…I'm just so sorry about Kyle."

"Thank you. Promise me you'll be careful."

"I promise."

Christine went directly to the address Rolf gave her and delivered his message. She knew that she was fairly safe during the daylight, but she still felt as if she were being followed. *I'm just being silly, there's no sense worrying about it now.* When she got home, she realized that she hadn't eaten in nearly two days. She ordered some Chinese food but fell asleep with a box of rice in her hands. She immediately fell into the dream about the ritual again. First, she was lying on the altar, then it was Leah. They mixed her blood with Leah's as their chanting became more and more intense. The hooded figure in the front was part man and part beast. As he drank the blood mixture, he looked directly at her, but it seemed more like he was looking through her. She turned her head and was awakened by the sound of her phone ringing. She was dripping sweat and had spilled Chinese all over her.

It took several moments for her to slow her heart rate. Her hands shook as she attempted to answer the call. It was the hospital. The dayshift doctor let her know that a woman had stopped by asking about a woman who fit Leah's description. The doctor had told her that he couldn't release any information about the patient unless she was a direct relative.

"I'll be there in half an hour. Don't let anyone near her," Christine ordered.

"I'll call in extra staff so that someone is with her at all times."

"Perfect thank you."

"Oh, and Dr. Rodgers, they are holding a body in the morgue, waiting for you. They said that you wanted to attend the autopsy."

"Yes, I will take care of that. Thank you. I'll be there shortly." She dressed quickly and went down to hail a cab.

Rolf awoke before dusk and got ready to take the letter Christine had brought over to Victor. The parchment looked as if it may even be older than the book. Hopefully it was the piece to the puzzle they needed. Victor and the others were already waiting for Rolf when he arrived. There was a man present who Rolf had never seen before. He found it strange that no introductions were made. The man took the letter and placed it on the desk under a bright lamp. Silence fell upon the room as the man studied the letter and began writing notes. There was nothing for him to do at the moment, so Rolf told Victor that he would be at the club if he needed anything.

The club was overflowing with new faces. William came up to him and handed him a drink.

"Has Tristin been in tonight?"

"Yes, she's in the back with some guy I've never seen before."

"I have a feeling I know who it is. I'm going to join them. I'll check in with you before I leave," Rolf said.

As he approached the table, Colin was first to notice him.

"Brother, how are you?"

"What do you care?"

"Come on, Rolf. You don't have to be like that. We can just let things go back to the way they were."

"Not in this lifetime." Tristin stood up and planted a kiss on Rolf's cheek. He tried to pull away, but she just released him and laughed.

"Join us, Rolf."

"I think I will." Rolf could tell by the look on his brother's face that he was shocked he had accepted the offer. Colin scooted down the booth a little to make room and asked the cocktail waitress to bring another round.

Rolf sat, "So, what did I interrupt?" he asked.

"Nothing, just old friends catching up."

"You were away for a while, weren't you? Out of the country, I heard," Rolf said.

"Your human pet kept you well informed," she hissed.

"Why'd you kill him Tristin? He was no threat to you."

"Oh Rolf, I was just trying to save you from yourself."

"I don't need anything from you."

"Maybe not now, but you will. I assure you of that."

"I would rather die than ever need you for anything again." In a rage, Rolf got up and left the club. He felt sick to his stomach with hate for that vile woman. If it was the last thing he ever did, he would make sure that Christine was kept safe. He had to be careful. If either Tristin or Colin caught wind of his feelings for Christine, it would be equivalent to signing her death warrant. He was nowhere near ready to experience all of that again.

Back at the table, Colin told Tristin about Rolf's frequent visits to the hospital and about the night that he saw him with the doctor.

"I think it would be wise to do some checking around on her."

"Take care of that for me, will you? And make it soon, the time is almost here. You won't forget our deal?"

"Of course not, Tristin."

Chapter Thirty-One

Christine was on her way back to work. Going over the events of the previous night kept her mind busy. She had always believed in the dark world, but to know that it actually existed was both frightening and fascinating. She paid the cab driver and walked toward the entrance. A man suddenly stepped out of the shadows; she recognized him as the man she saw Rolf talking to the other night.

"Doctor, may I have a moment of your time?"

"Of course, but only a moment. I really must get to my rounds."

"I am looking for a young woman—sixteen, maybe younger?

"Do you have her name?"

"I don't."

"Then you aren't a relative?"

"No, I'm a private investigator."

"I'm sorry, sir. Patient information is restricted to anyone but direct family."

"Thank you for your time doctor,"

"Sorry I couldn't be of more help."

Christine went straight to Leah's room and found her highly agitated. She called for an orderly, "When was she sedated last?". She turned around to see a new orderly standing in the doorway.

"Can I be of any help?" the orderly asked.

"No, I'm sorry, I was looking for Max. He is very familiar with her dosing schedule."

"He went to the medicine room."

"That's fine. I'll wait. This room is off limits to new hires. Authorized personnel only on this case I'm afraid."

"Of course, sorry about that." He walked away and Christine called down to security to ask about the new orderly. He sent off a strange alarm in her head. The guard confirmed that he started just a few days ago.

"Well, I don't want him in my ward," Christine told the guard.

"Yes, ma'am."

"Thank you." Christine finished her rounds and headed to her office. She was unsettled to find the door ajar. She knew she had closed it. She entered the room cautiously. It seemed nothing was missing. She jumped when her office phone rang. It was the guard letting her know that she had a visitor. Rolf offered her a gentle smile as she approached the gate.

"I don't have time for coffee today, but I really want to discuss something with you," she told him. Once they were seated in her office she continued, "Do you remember the man you were talking to a few nights ago?"

"Yes. His name is Colin. Why?"

"He stopped me on my way in tonight and asked me about Leah. He didn't know her name or anything else about her besides that he thought she was about sixteen. I just told him that I couldn't discuss patient information with someone who wasn't family. He seemed to understand."

"Good. And he left you alone after that?"

"Yes. Is he like you?"

"Yes. Except, you can't trust him. He's involved in the awakening. He wants to see you all destroyed."

"I know. I could feel the evil in him. How does he know about me and Leah?"

"I honestly don't know."

"Another thing, there is a new orderly who totally gives me the creeps. He was hanging out around her room, insisting he help with her medications. I already requested that security keep him out of the isolation ward altogether."

"Smart. Well, listen, keep me posted. I have to meet with Victor, but I will share this information with him. Stay alert Christine. You're doing a great job here. If you need me, call."

"I will. Thanks Rolf."

As Rolf was leaving the hospital, he immediately saw Colin waiting across the street.

"Well, well, well. Fancy meeting you here," Colin smirked.

"So, you are stalking me?"

"Who is the doctor to you, Rolf?"

"None of your damn business."

"You should really learn to stick with your own kind, brother."

Colin left to find Tristin. She was disappointed that he didn't have much to report. Meanwhile, Rolf made it back to Victor's with about three hours until dawn.

"I'm afraid we have some bad news for you Rolf," Victor said, leading him into the library.

"What have you found out?"

"Dr. Rodgers and the young girl are to be used as the human sacrifices to wake the queen."

"No. There must be something we can do."

"We are doing everything in our power to figure it out, son."

"But we are running out of time."

"I know. Stay as near to them as you can without causing suspicion."

"Of course."

"Rolf, I need you to be prepared to do whatever is necessary."

"Absolutely. Anything."

Rolf left and stopped by the club briefly. He wanted to check on William and grab a couple of bottles of blood. Colin was still there with Tristin and another woman that Rolf didn't recognize. *Maybe she's a slave*, he thought. *Come to think of it, I haven't seen her last slave since she's been back. I wonder what she did to her.*

Chapter Thirty-Two

Back at Victor's home, the watchers were able to translate more of the letter. They knew that they had to get this information back to Rolf right away. Unfortunately, with the sun peaking over the mountain tops, it would have to wait until sundown. Victor requested that additional watchers be placed at the hospital and around Dr. Rodger's home.

Christine made her final rounds and decided to sit with Leah for a little while before going home. The girl was in the middle of what seemed like a terrible dream. She kept muttering a phrase under her breath, but it was in a language that Christine didn't recognize. She tried to write down the words as best she should. She knew that Rolf would be able to help her decipher the message.

Christine hailed a cab to go home. As they were driving past the old bookstore, she saw that the door was open. She immediately asked the cabby to pull over, threw some money at him, and jumped out of the car. She entered the store and noticed that the same clerk was standing behind the counter. He met her eyes and motioned for her to follow him to the back of the store. He led her the section on ancient texts, then returned to his post at the front. She immediately noticed a book that was sticking out about an inch or so past all the rest. She could tell that it had recently been moved because the dust on the shelf had been disturbed. With the book in hand, she turned around and noticed that the store had vanished. She was standing in the empty warehouse with the closed sign still sitting in the window. She rushed to the door praying that she hadn't been locked in. She felt like she couldn't get away fast enough. She threw open the door and ran out to the cab, that she was grateful was still waiting for her. She gave the cabby directions to Victor's house.

She tried to reach Rolf on the phone but kept getting his voicemail. Once she arrived at Victor's, she knocked persistently on the door until someone answered. Surprised to see her, he invited her in. She told him about the experience that she had just had and gave him the book. She ended up falling asleep on the couch in Victor's library. When she awoke, she had a message from Rolf that he wanted to see her as soon as it was dark. She sent him a message back, letting him know that she would be at the hospital.

Rolf didn't even have to knock when he arrived. Victor opened it immediately and let him in.

"It's close Rolf."

"I know. I can feel it."

"The doctor brought a new book over this morning. It's even older than the first. This must be the work of someone who wants us to stop this from happening."

"But why all the mystery?"

"I don't know."

"I'll stop by there on my way to the hospital and poke around a little bit—see what I can find."

"Excellent idea."

"I'll be in touch, Victor."

Rolf arrived at the bookstore and found a way in through the back. He noticed two sets of footprints in the dust on the floor, leading to the back of the warehouse. He found the ancient texts shelf and could immediately see where the first two books had been removed. He noticed a third book sticking out a little bit and grabbed it. He turned around a noticed a shadow moving out the door. By the time Rolf had reached the alley, the shadow was gone. There was absolutely no sign of movement whatsoever. He secured the book in his coat pocket, then decided that he had time to stop by the club and check on William before meeting Christine at the hospital.

He dropped the third book off with Victor and flew to the club. William seemed to be a little out of sorts when he arrived.

"Is something the matter?"

"Two of our mortal regulars have gone missing. I can't find them anywhere.

"Keep looking and call me if there's any more trouble." Rolf went up to the office and poured himself a double. He stood at the large window that overlooked the club but didn't see anything that would cause concern. He finished his bookwork and left for the hospital to see Christine.

Christine was just about to leave for her shift when she got a phone call from the hospital. Leah was missing. She ran down the stairs and hailed a cab. She gave him directions to the hospital and asked him to please hurry. A minute later, the cabby made a wrong turn. She tried to knock on the window to get his attention, but he wouldn't turn around; he just kept driving. She looked at the photo of the man in the license that was posted and realized that this was not the man that was driving. Panic set in as she tried to unlock the door and roll down the window. She was trapped. They drove for over an hour to a very old and rundown part of the city. The cabby pulled up in front of an ancient looking castle or fortress of some kind. She remembered reading about sites like this that were used in the War of Independence. She suddenly remembered that she still had her cell phone on her, but they were so far out in the middle of nowhere that finding a signal was impossible.

The man came around and opened her door. Seeing him face to face she immediately recognized him; it was Colin.

"Don't struggle okay. It will only make things harder on you," he told her. Tristin walked up to her and Christine felt a wave of nausea. This woman radiated evil like a nuclear bomb.

"So, you're the one who has captured Rolf's heart this time. He is always falling for the wrong women," Tristin hissed at her. "He's mine and he always will be, or he will die."

"Why are you doing this?"

"You wouldn't understand."

"Try me," Christine challenged. Tristin only laughed and told Colin to bring her to the dungeon.

"Make sure she remains unharmed until the time is right," Tristin added laughing.

"I'm sorry that you got dragged into this doctor," Colin said quietly as he led Christine away.

"If you're sorry, then let me go."

"I can't do that. Don't let that pretty face fool you. She is really unpleasant when she's angry."

"Oh really? And I thought she was like that all the time."

"I like you doctor," Colin laughed. "But, I can't help you. And I wouldn't hold your breath for Rolf either. He's always been two steps behind Tristin."

"Did you help her kill Rolf's friends?"

"No, I don't have the same taste for blood the way she does. Usually, I don't have to use such force. By the time I am ready to kill they will do anything for me, even die willingly."

"You are worse than she is. At least with her there is no false charm. What you see is what you get." Colin threw his head back and laughed at her comment.

"You know, your precious Rolf was just like me. The three of us were always together."

"What happened?

"Tristin became more…aggressive, in her kills and Rolf just didn't have the stomach for it I guess.

"And you do?"

"This lifestyle isn't for everyone. Particularly not mortals."

"I can see that."

"So will Rolf, in time." Colin took her down a dark hallway and led her into the first cell. He chained her to the wall, then left for a moment. He returned with a blanket. "It's going to get cold down here. Have a nice night doctor."

When she was sure he was gone, Christine tried to figure out how to get free, but it was no use. Those old chains were still a lot stronger than they looked. The chain was just long enough for her to be able to sit down. She couldn't see a thing, but she could hear some sort of creature scurrying through the cellar. *Rats*, she guessed. *If I survive this, I swear I will never lock up another patient again.*

Chapter Thirty-Three

When Rolf arrived at the hospital, there were several police cars out front. As soon as he got off the elevator, he was stopped by a uniformed officer. Dr. Rodgers' orderly rushed over and told the cop to let Rolf through.

"Sir, Dr. Rodgers has been missing for the last two hours. Any idea of her whereabouts?"

"My God…"

"Her patient, Leah, has also been taken. Do you know anything about that?"

"I'm sorry sir, I don't know anything. I'm going to look for her. Here is my card. I will be in touch if I find her," Rolf shouted as he took off running back down the hall. Rolf called Victor.

"They have them. They've already taken Christine and Leah."

"We've got to find them Rolf."

"I'm going back to the club now. I know Colin and Tristin have them, I just need to find out where they are."

"Keep me posted." Victor said before Rolf ended the call. As soon as he arrived at the club, William told Rolf that Colin and Tristin hadn't been in tonight.

"But, there were several vampires that I have never seen before and a lot of talk about the moon and some kind of ceremony." Rolf knew he had less than forty-eight hours to find them. His mind raced as panic set in over the gravity of the situation. Back at Victor's, the watchers were working around the clock to try to make a breakthrough on the books and their translations. They had maps of the city and were trying to narrow down spots that could be used for a ritual of this magnitude.

Rolf dreamt of a man named Nicolai. Rolf was fighting for the American's and Nicolai was a spy for the British. They were both secretly vampires and both equally as skilled with a sword. They met for the first time on the battlefield. Nicolai got the upper hand for a moment, and was about to cut off Rolf's head, when Tristin stopped him and told him to leave. She looked at Rolf and asked him when he was going to stop fighting on the wrong side; then she was gone.

Rolf awoke with a start. He hadn't even realized that he had fallen asleep. He got up and heard a loud knocking at the door. It wasn't quite dark outside yet, but the hallway was sufficiently shaded. It was the detectives from the hospital.

"Do you have any news on Dr. Rodgers?" Rolf asked them.

"No, but we need you to come down to the station's morgue. We have a few bodies for you to look at to see if one of them is the missing woman."

"I'll get dressed and be right out." Rolf knew that it wasn't going to be Christine and Leah. He knew that Tristin needed to keep them alive for a little while longer. It wasn't time yet.

Rolf arrived at Victor's just as they were finishing the final translation.

"It sounds like they will awaken Thomas first, then take him to wherever they are holding Christine and Leah. Tristin and two other Elders of her same status will also have to be there. The blood of the child will be mixed with Thomas' and that of the other Elders, then they will mix it with Christine's. This will then be transferred to the queen. It will be a slow process. We have a very small margin of opportunity, but at least we have one. Rolf, Christine will have to be turned. That is our only hope of stopping this madness."

"That can't be the only way."

"You said you would be prepared to do anything Rolf."

"Yes, but…"

"If you can't do it, then I will." Victor roared. Rolf felt faint. He sworn to himself that he would never turn another. That's the whole reason why he had opened the club in the first place.

"I'll do it," Rolf said in a barely audible whisper. He suddenly remembered his dream from last night. It had taken place during the War of Independence. "I think I know where they are. There is an old fortress in old New York, where they held prisoners during the War of Independence. I dreamt of the place last night. It would be perfect for this kind of thing."

"Okay, let's split up. Half of us will go to Thomas' awakening and follow them, the other half of you, head to the fortress and see if you can locate the girls." Victor ordered. "Be alert everyone. Good luck."

Christine didn't know if it was day or night. She was cold and hungry and her bones hurt from shivering for hours on end. She suddenly heard someone coming down the hall. She saw the glow of a pale light and then recognized the frail frame of Leah. They were carrying her. Christine searched for any sign of life in the girl. She hung limp in the man's arms. Her thoughts turned to Rolf, and she prayed that he would find them before it was too late. Colin followed the man carrying Leah. He stopped in front of her cell and told her that they would be coming for her soon.

"For what?"

"Better not say, doctor. Wouldn't want to ruin the surprise."

Not far away, the ceremony to awaken Thomas was underway. The queen's casket was already waiting at the fortress. The altar had been prepared and the Elders were in their places. Tristin thought, *finally, I will have everything I always wanted. Except maybe Rolf, but this sacrifice will be worth the outcome.* She was looking forward to seeing Thomas again; she had missed him. He was probably the only one, besides Colin, who truly understood her.

Rolf arrived at the fortress site and knew that his hunch had been correct. There was a lot of movement within the walls of the ruined building. He silently made his way down one of the corridors and knocked out a guard, taking his robes as a disguise. He made his way down to the dungeon but it appeared he was too late. He could smell a trace of human scent in the air. It was a bit stronger on the blanket he found lying near the shackles, but Christine and Leah were nowhere to be found. He heard footsteps and ducked behind a pillar until a man and woman passed him by. They joined a small group of vampires standing nearby. As the group began to move down the corridor to a large room in the center of the fortress, Rolf silently eased along with them. The room held a large altar at the front, recreated for this specific ritual. Leah was restrained at one side, while Christine lay shackled on the other. Rolf got as close to Christine as he could without being detected. He wished that he could reassure her, to let her know that he was near, but he didn't want to draw attention to her or himself.

Just then, Thomas entered the room with Tristin and Colin. The other Elders followed not far behind. Rolf spotted Victor and some of the other watchers in a group also entering the room. Rolf could almost hear the blood rushing through his veins. His heart only beat faster as all of this came to a head. A few of the slaves opened what was left of the shutters and let the moonlight shine through the vacant window spaces. The eclipse was beginning. Drums began to pound rhythmically, echoing off the walls of the chamber. Thomas was handed an ancient chart to read, while others continued to fill the room.

The queen lay between the two sacrifices. Leah had an IV inserted into her arm. Thomas initiated the transfer. The chanting grew louder as the life blood of the young girl was removed from her body. Rolf began to move forward, but Victor signaled him to wait. It was clear that both women couldn't be saved. As Leah's blood flowed through Thomas to Queen Lucia, the queen began to transform. She took on the appearance of a younger and very beautiful woman—even more beautiful than Tristin. Leah, on the other hand was pale as a ghost. *At least she isn't suffering*, Rolf thought. As the last drop of her blood flowed through the tube and into the queen, the noise level in the room became deafening. Thomas raised his arms to silence the crowd. Then, he turned and slowly approached Christine.

Rolf anxiously watched Victor for the signal to move. Doing nothing was excruciating. Thomas inserted the IV in her arm himself. Rolf could see the fear in her eyes from where he stood. By chance, her eyes fluttered to the corner of the room and met his. When they did, he could tell that she instantly calmed. The chanting in the room grew loud again. Rolf could see various watchers around the room subtly moving into place. They had one chance, and one chance only, to get this right.

The moon was almost completely covered by this time, and the excitement in the room had reached the level of a roar again. The queen was beginning to stir, as Christine became more and more ashen. Rolf made his move as Victor simultaneously sent a stake through Thomas' heart. Across the room, two other watchers were making the same attack on Tristin and Colin. Rolf took Christine in his arms, and as gently as he could, sunk his fangs into her vulnerable neck. He felt what little warmth was left in her body rush through him. She felt his life energy reinvigorate every inch of her. He was afraid that he had waited too long to act, but she opened her eyes and gazed at him without fear. She kissed him with a passion that she'd restrained for the last few weeks.

Victor took control of the room and became the head Elder of the coven for the next two hundred years. For good measure, Victor stabbed the queen through the heart to ensure that she would never wake again.

Rolf carried Christine into the night, and they lived happily forever after.

The End

THE SHIP WITH BLACK SAILS

Prologue

Ireland 1824

Dressed in black, she floated silently down the servant's stairs. Two shadows, standing in the tree line, fell in step behind her as she passed by.

In a matter of minutes, they reached the hidden cove that only she, her crew and her grandmother knew. She was Raven O'Malley Fitzgerald, only granddaughter of the Duchess of Blackthorn. Raven upheld her grandmother's tradition of helping the downtrodden people of Ireland. Forty years earlier, an infamous pirate captained a ship painted red. The villainous crew harassed and plundered the fleet of the East India Company. The crown of England offered a 500-pound bounty for the capture of the mysterious pirate.

Captain Andrew Fitzgerald, heir to the Duke of Blackthorn, was assigned the task of hunting down the notorious pirate. Little did he know, upon capturing his prey, he would find his one true love. There began the love story of his lifetime. Only a handful of people knew what became of the notorious buccaneer - her devoted husband, son and granddaughter.

Raven had ordered her first mate and childhood friend, Michael Fitz, to have her grandmother's ship painted midnight black.

Chapter One

London 1824 Two Weeks Earlier

"Raven! I've had enough," the Duke of Summerset yelled at his impetuous daughter. The Marques, heir to the Duke of Blackthorn and his wife, tried for years to find and secure a suitable match for their daughter yet she'd just walked out on her groom in the middle of the ceremony. "You're going back to Ireland! Not even your grandparents can save you this time! Have Jane pack your things. And these wretched books your grandmother gives you, they are staying here! Go! Now! You will bring no more disgrace upon this family." He shook his head and murmured to no one in particular, *if only she could be more like Robert.*

As Raven headed up the long staircase she found her grandmother waiting. The Duchess wrapped her arms around her granddaughter and the two burst into laughter and scurried up the stairs. When safely in her room they stood at the window watching the busy market in Mayfair.

"Are you still bent on this course?" the Duchess asked.

"Yes grandmother, I'm ready. This mustn't be postponed any longer. The people of Ireland are starving," Raven replied.

"You know it's best to keep this from your grandfather. He's gotten stuffy in his old age." They hugged one another in a hasty goodbye.

Ireland 1824

Off the coast of Ireland, a ferocious battle raged between the *Falcon*, a British Man O War and the *Hawk*, a pirate vessel. The British were fighting for their lives; their commandant, Alexander, was covered in blood. He wasn't sure if it was his or that of the man he'd run through with his sword. But the pirates were gaining the upper hand. A gunshot rang out. A musket ball knocked Alexander off his feet. As he fell, his second-in-command raised the white flag.

As Alexander Knight of the Viscount Craven opened his eyes, a giant of a pirate towered over him, blood-stained sword raised. He heard only the cannon's blast, signaling a return of arms. The pirates vacated the tattered British ship.

Silently, a black vessel crept around the bow of the disabled British ship. Raven stood at the helm ordering her crew to render aid to the survivors. "There will be time to pursue the perpetrators later." She knew the pirate John Bryce waylaid the British vessel. The same man razed several Irish villages. The same pirate killed Michael's older brother and forced the survivors of his village into press gangs.

Many of the pirate bodies strewn upon the deck of the British ship were those very men. Raven was not out for the same noble reason Sky had followed so many years earlier but Sky gave her granddaughter her blessing for the mission, that, in her mind, was justice.

Raven knew the British ship well. It was Alexander's *Falcon*. She'd lived next door to the Knight family all her life. Alex never gave Raven even the slightest look while she spent her days fantasizing about him. He was part of the reason she had left her groom at the altar.

When Raven knelt beside Alex's unconscious body she worried over his stillness. Gone was his imposing posture, here lie a mortal, vulnerable man. As she finished dressing his wounds he began to open his eyes. Concerned he would see through her disguise she busied herself gathering bloody cloths and her field service kit, "My doctor is assisting yours in caring for your injured and disposing of the deceased."

"Who are you?" he asked.

"Just the captain of a passing ship. We stopped to render aid per protocol."

"Only outlaws hide their identity," he insisted.

Raven laughed as she swung back to her ship. By this time there was no sign of the pirates.

Raven decided to go back to the cove. She hated to leave Alex but she knew it wouldn't be long before another British ship arrived.

Chapter Two

Raven got out of her bath. Her hair had returned to its natural color and she was now able to put her thick glasses back on. She had a lot of practice navigating with them on. The lenses were slightly colored so that her vibrant emerald eyes weren't as noticeable. All of her life she had lived in her disguise because she refused to conform to her parent's expectations – not that they ever noticed. Even her grandfather didn't really see her for who she was. Her grandmother was the only one who recognized her for who she really was. Besides her crew. Her grandmother was the only one who understood her.

Raven gazed out her window where she was startled to see two British frigates, towing the Man O War, so soon. She rushed to get dressed, making sure that she was presentable. By the time she arrived downstairs, the butler was announcing Alex's arrival in the foyer, along with two other officers that were being carried in. Raven took charge and sent for the doctor, who resided in the back of the castle. She assessed the wounds of the men herself while the housekeeper and the cook tried to chase her out of the room – reminding her that her behavior was improper.

Just as Raven was preparing her protest, the doctor came rushing in. He attended to Alex first, as protocol warranted as he was the highest-ranking officer. Dr. Meyrick spent over six hours treating the wounded. Raven ordered tea and lunch for them all and saw that food was sent to the wounded crew still on the ship as well.

Chapter Three

Raven sat by Alex's side round the clock, letting her staff take over the rest of her duties. Three days after the battle, Alex woke to the sound of a husky whisper. His first thought was, *I don't even know your name.*

Seeing the confusion on his face, she slowly walked over to him and said, "Alex, it's me, Raven."

"But, I heard her voice. She saved our lives, and I didn't even get her name," he muttered. Watching him fall back into a natural sleep, Raven was relieved that there was no fever present. She was going to have to be more careful. It hurt that he was thinking of the masked woman and not her, but after all, that is what needed to be to keep her identity safe.

London

Admiral Gage convened with Captain Joshua Steele and Baron Von to discuss the dire importance of the renegade, Captain Bryce, being stopped.

"I won't stand for another attack on one of our ships!" The Admiral exclaimed. "Has there been any word on Knight? His family wants results"

"The last I heard, he was giving the Lady Raven fits. Those two are forever at odds," Steele answered.

"Any word on the ship that rescued them:" Admiral Gage asked.

"No Admiral, the reports are sketchy at best," Baron Von said.

"The fact is, it is reported to be a woman with a wicked sword arm. The ship is all black and the captain dressed in black with a silk mask over her face," Steele offered.

Admiral Gage was quiet for a moment. He then called his petty officer and told him to get the Duke of Blackthorn at once. The Baron lifted his eyebrows at Steele; both men remained quiet. The Duke was a legend in their circle. He had been the youngest commandant ever and was known as a master swordsman.

Chapter Four

The winter sun left the rocky coast in a red haze as it set. Raven met her companions at their normal spot. John Bryce hit another village that morning, killing several men and taking the rest – women included. He'd been sighted at the cove just west of her location. As she and her crew sailed out of the cove, her thoughts centered on her aggravated house guest. Raven had to focus on her mission; she would have to strike fast. Bryce was creating quite a name for himself. He had to be stopped as soon as possible.

On Bryce's ship, they were celebrating another victory. His men had presented him with the comeliest wench in the village. Her screams could be heard throughout every inch of the ship.

Raven wasn't able to locate her prey, so she returned to the cove just before dawn. She forced herself to go back to her rooms. She wanted to check on Alex, but she had to wash the color out of her hair first.

Raven made her way to Alex's side just as the household started stirring. He woke to another dream about the mysterious captain who saved him. He heard the door open and watched as Raven entered. Alex noticed that she looked tired and distracted. *Just once, I would like to see her in a fashionable gown, without her spectacles and that severe hairstyle,* he thought to himself. Raven seem so self-assured when no one was looking – as if she knew a secret that no one else knew.

Alex looks more himself today, Raven thought. *Hopefully, he will soon be ready to leave.* His ship was almost ready to sail again and his injured men healed and rested.

Chapter Five

Bryce was pacing around his cabin. It had been reported that a female captain had been asking an awful lot of questions about him. His thoughts took him back to the time he served under Captain Fitzgerald, the present Duke of Blackthorn. Unfortunately, they had a falling out over the elusive female pirate, Sky O'Malley. Without much of a skirmish Fitzgerald and crew had captured O'Malley. Captain Fitzgerald had the captain of the *Liberator* taken to his cabin where he treated her wounds and nursed her back to health. As she mended she freely walked about the decks, unsupervised. She had captured the imagination of the crew, all admired her courage and beauty but she only had eyes for Fitzgerald. It was evident Fitzgerald held in her in the highest regard and took great pleasure in her company. She remained his cabin mate throughout the ship's sailing.

The close relationship between captains proved especially vexing to John Bryce. He harbored a growing jealously and became driven to make Sky his own. One evening, late, Sky couldn't sleep so she threw on a light dressing gown and set out to enjoy the salty night air. She leaned against the ship's rail, letting the sea breeze caress her face. Bryce's evening routine had become lurking outside the captain's cabin, lusting after Sky, trying to devise the means of getting her for himself when he spotted her leaving the cabin. He followed her, unsure of his course of action but sure she would be his that night. As she stood against the rails, eyes closed, he snuck up behind her and struck her with the butt of his pistol. He took her to the hold, brutally raped and beat her. He left her, thinking to return later and ravish her again.

When Fitzgerald awoke the next morning, Sky was nowhere to be found.

After hours of searching, he finally found her in the hold of his ship, half dead. It didn't take him long to figure out who was responsible for her condition. Fitzgerald ordered that Bryce be whipped and set adrift in a long boat, with only water and a few days' worth of rations.

Bryce's awareness came back to the present moment as he pressed is fingers to his temple. Sky was the reason he took such pleasure in attacking the Irish coast. In his mind, it was revenge against the high and mighty Duke.

Chapter Six

London

Hundreds of miles away, Sky was also awake, standing in front of the window and looking out over the Thymes River. Her thoughts, too, drifted back to that day when she'd been brutally attacked. When the Duke found her gazing out the window, he knew what she had just been reliving in her mind's eye. He held her until she was able to control her shaking. He gently took her face in his hands, gazed sincerely into her eyes and told her how much he loved her.

Ireland 1824

Raven woke up from another dream of Alex. She wished that he would leave because, even if he came to return her feelings, she knew she would never be able to marry a peer of the realm. This hit Raven hard because she was sure there was no other man for her. This brought her thoughts back to Bryce – the man who was probably her real grandfather. She had found her grandmother's journals right before the wedding and that was why she felt compelled to leave her groom at the altar.

There were several scores to settle with Bryce. Raven had never asked Sky about the things written in her journal. If the town found out, it would ruin her brother and father. Little did she know, that had she read just a little further, there would be one less reason for revenge.

Alex was having another dream about the mysterious captain of the black ship. When she approached him, she resembled Raven but dark hair flowed about her waist and emerald eyes held him awestruck, so unlike Raven's harsh hairstyle and glasses. He had never seen her like this in all the time he's known her. Alex found himself starting to reach for her, but the scene before him quickly transformed into the battle – his men dying all around him. He saw the pirate's sword coming at him and, at the last moment, another sword deflected what would have been a fatal blow.

Raven gently roused Alex from his dreams, "There's an officer here to see you, from the Admiralty." Just then, Josh Steele pushed into the room, a grave look etched into his face. With one look he dismissed Raven. She quietly closed the door, allowing them privacy in their conversation.

As soon as she'd left the room he approached Alex, the two men shook hands, "I hear you had a go with that vermin Bryce."

"Yes, it's true. He nearly got the best of me. Had it not been for the ghostly lady captain I might not be here to welcome you. It's good to see you Josh."

"I come as the bearer of sad news." Josh shared the purpose of his mission, "The Duke of Blackthorn's son and grandson were murdered in their home four days ago. His Grace couldn't get here himself and requested that you break the news to Lady Raven. He's also requested that you get back to London as soon as you are able."

"My ship isn't quite ready."

"I brought the Duke's yacht. It's the fastest way."

"How do I share such news with Lady Raven? I've know her all her life," Alex asked solemnly.

"I know that there is a lot of discontent between you, but it will still come as a blow no matter who the words come from," Josh answered honestly. "Especially because she must now consider that she will become the next duchess."

Chapter Seven

Raven walked along the gardens wondering why the family yacht was here. Despite her curiosity, she wasn't quite ready to return to the castle. Michael had sent word that her prey had been spotted in London, at the docks. She was starting to get a bad feeling in the pit of her stomach. Her grandmother called feelings like this 'second sight'.

Alex paced the floor as he mulled over how to break the dreadful news to Raven. Suddenly, the door burst open and she marched into his room. Her hair was windblown, her face red from the crisp morning air. Before he could start his rehearsed speech, she looked him dead in the eye and demanded to know what had happened. He was taken aback by her manner and thought that she was every inch a Duchess in this moment.

Alex looked like he would rather be anywhere else at that moment.

"Raven, I've received some bad news from London…." he began, but she cut him off.

"No…no, not my grandparents!" Alex was taken aback by the sheer terror that claimed her eyes and caused her voice to tremble.

"No, no my lady. There was a shooting at your father's home. He and your brother have been murdered…that's all I know for now, except that I will bring you safely to your family. I am so sorry for your loss.

"I'll be ready to sail with the tide. If you are not feeling well enough, I have men that will join me," she said confidently. *She is being so brave*, he thought. As brave as the woman in his dreams.

"Your grandfather left your care to me Raven. It is my duty to take you and keep you safe." A part of her was thrilled, but the other part of her was annoyed, she was the one who had saved his life, after all.

Chapter Eight

Raven made her way down the secret passage way to meet with Michael. She was going to have him take her ship to a secret cove near London and find out what he could about her prey. It couldn't be a random coincidence that Bryce was spotted in London at the same time her family was murdered. It didn't make any sense for him to kill his own son and grandson though. Raven felt confusion, hurt, and anger course through her veins.

She made the short walk back to the castle; completely unaware she was being watched. The man turned and quietly walked away with any indication that he had been there in the first place.

Alex also watched her. He thought about going to her but knew his presence would only make her uncomfortable. Despite this, he felt compelled to make sure that she understood he was there for her.

Chapter Nine

Raven had trouble sleeping that night. Her thoughts were being divided between the man who slept down the hall, and the man she vowed to kill. She had never really had a close relationship with her father and brother, but they were blood. If there was one thing that her grandparents pounded into her head it was that family comes first.

Alex laid wide awake at least an hour before dawn. His heart went out the brave woman down the hall. He could hear her pacing several times throughout the night but didn't know how to help her. Alex couldn't put his finger on when she had become this courageous young woman. He found that this discovery left him feeling both uncomfortable and intrigued. She had always been the little brat that followed him and Miles around. Miles, Alex's older brother by two years, was the patient one. He's always stood up for Raven. They would sit and talk for hours about the sea. Alex knew that she had been raised sailing on the Duke's yacht. By the time she was ten or twelve years old, she told everyone that she was the captain. Miles always used to give her a big salute, humoring her accomplishment, while Alex never saw her as anything more than a pest.

When he made his way downstairs, he was surprised to find Raven ready to go.

"Good morning my lady. I hope that the day finds you well," Alex greeted her politely. Raven shot him a haughty look. He couldn't believe how much she looked like her grandmother at this moment. He used to love to sit and talk to the Duchess. She'd always made the time for him whereas his own mother often could not be bothered.

"I'm as good as I can be under the circumstance," the sound of Raven's voice brought Alex back from his thoughts. "Shall we make way to the yacht?"

"Of course, my lady." They gathered their belongings and strolled towards the docks. After a few moments of silence between them, Alex blurted out, "You know, you don't always have to be so strong. It is perfectly acceptable to allow others to help you."

"Yes, Alex, I do have to be strong. Someone needs to be strong for my grandparents, and at this time the only person left is me."

"Raven, your grandparents are the strongest, most grounded people I know." Josh interrupted their conversation, "my lady, you look absolutely beautiful today," he offered after placing a delicate kiss on the top of her hand.

"Thank-you, Josh."

Josh noticed how Alex watched them out of the corner of his eye. If ever there had been two people better suited for one another, he didn't know them.

It was then that he decided to pay court to Lady Raven, just to tweak the nose of the high and mighty Alex Knight. For some reason, he enjoyed watching his friends fall into the noose of marriage but was sure to run as soon as the women of his family tried to mate him to some acceptable young woman. Josh wasn't quite as tall as Alex, but he was just as handsome.

As they made their way along the rough passageway, Alex thought about how much he loved this part of Ireland. His grandfather loved the southern coast of Ireland, but his father hated it. Cork had been his grandfather's home until the day he died. The great house had been sadly neglected over the years since his passing.

Raven stood at the bow of the ship, looking out to the sea. It was as if she came alive in the sea spray. Alex had a strange feeling that he knew her innermost thoughts at this moment. The feeling quickly left him when he noted the sadness in her eyes. Josh approached and offered Raven his arm. Raven found that she rather enjoyed how easy it was to flirt with him – whereas it was anything but with Alex. She often felt as though she could never say the right thing with Alex.

That night, they hit a bad storm. Alex couldn't do much as he was still weak and tired. Raven tied herself to the wheel and Josh stood behind her – together they kept on course.

Chapter Ten

The Duke and Duchess sat quietly at their table. Not a word was spoken, each of their thoughts taking different paths. Sky was thinking about the chest up in the attic. As soon as the Duke went to his club, she would go up there and confront her past. She prayed that Raven would be safe; however, she also knew that both Knight and Steele would die before ever letting her down. A subtle smile played across Sky's lips as she thought it a brilliant plan to send Josh along to retrieve Raven. Alex needed a little nudge toward her granddaughter. One day, they would see what she had seen for years.

As the Duke made his way to his club, he worried about what was left of his family. He should have ended this years ago. The night he found Sky beaten and raped crept into his thoughts. That was the worst night of his life. The second worst night of his life was but four nights ago when he learned of the murder of his son and grandson. He knew he wouldn't be able to live with himself if…no, he couldn't even finish the thought; it was totally unacceptable. As he looked around, he wondered where time had gone. His life had been so full, he'd often thought, *No one should be this happy*. They, of course, had their bad times too. He remembered the night Sky lost their second child. He'd almost lost her that night, too.

He'd finally reached White's, his favorite club. Several friends offered their condolences. Admiral Gage joined him at his table.

"Your Grace, they should arrive late afternoon or early evening. The storm has been brutal."

"I imagine that Raven is strapped to the wheel, shouting orders at everyone. I remember her sailing with us at just seven or eight, climbing the rigging like a monkey." Both men laughed at the memory.

Back at the ducal palace, Sky paced the attic. The diary containing her darkest secrets was gone. She contacted Sherman, her oldest friend and captain of her fleet. She'd always kept her "hands-on" style of running their shipping empire – much to her son's disgust. He'd felt strongly that she should step away from the command to let him handle the fleet. A fleet where Raven would carry on in their legacy – if they survived this latest ordeal.

Chapter Eleven

The storm had finally blown itself out. Raven could feel every muscle in her body aching, but she refused to let anyone else have the wheel yet. This was her favorite time at sea. There was a certain satisfaction to knowing that she beat Mother Nature. Alex awoke to another dream about the mysterious captain. This one had been the most vivid yet. He had taken her into his arms and ravished her mouth. When she broke away, it was Raven who stood in his arms. He sat up, startled. He wondered how she had managed to weasel her way into his dreams. It was bad enough that she had taken over his days. They made port in London at six o'clock that evening. There was a black coach bearing the Duke of Blackthorn's crest awaiting their arrival. Servants swarmed the deck to retrieve their luggage. Josh bid them a good evening and headed to the Admiralty. Alex could handle getting Raven home.

Raven was quiet during all of the hustle and bustle – not at all the competent woman she had been during the storm. In hindsight, Alex decided this was why he had dreamt of both women. He needed to get her to her family and go visit his mistress. Although, to his surprise, he was not all that anxious to see Lily even after weeks of separation.

Alex found himself standing outside of Lily's house. It didn't feel right, so he changed direction and headed for White's. When he entered, several of his peers came to see how he was doing. It wasn't long until the maître d' approached. He informed Alex that the Duke of Blackthorn and Admiral Gage requested that he join them at their private table.

"I presume my granddaughter is safe," the duke indicated that the waiter should pour Alex a brandy.

"Of course, sir."

"Please, call me Blackthorn."

Alex gave him a salute in response.

"Sirs, I am truly sorry that Bryce got away. We were caught off guard. It won't happen again," Alex lowered his eyes.

"I'm sure it won't," Blackthorn gave Alex a comforting pat on the shoulder. Alex wasn't so sure, but he knew he couldn't say so aloud.

So, tell us about this woman, Captain," the Admiral inquired.

"Well, sir, but for her, none of us would have made it. Her ship was painted black and it had black sails. The captain herself wore black. Half her face was covered. The instant Bryce's blade fell towards my head she intervened to save my life."

Changing the subject, Blackthorn asked, "My granddaughter wasn't too much trouble, now was she?"

"No sir, she was no trouble at all. She was rather amazing during the storm, actually." Alex admitted.

The conversation turned to other things, the men so engaged they failed to notice the man watching from the shadows.

Chapter Twelve

It had cost Derrick several pounds to get a membership to this club. He hated to do it, but his family's very lives depended on him. He, too, hated John Bryce. There was a time when he, the duke, and Bryce had been chums. And now, he owed his soul to that devil, Bryce. He didn't want to hurt Blackthorn any further but he had no choice. Thirty years ago, he was caught cheating at cards while he smoked opium and cheated on his wife. He blew through his inheritance and lost all of his property. Derrick mentally shook himself; he needed to stay focused.

He walked slowly out of the shadows towards Blackthorn.

"Your grace, it has been too long," he purred.

"Derrick, how good to see you," Blackthorn shook his hand warmly, genuinely glad to see his old chum. "It has been too long. You know Admiral Gage."

"Yes, of course," he shook the Admiral's hand and nodded in Alex's direction. "Gentlemen, forgive my disruption but I wanted to offer his grace my condolences."

"Of course, Derrick. Thank you. Let us see each other again soon and catch up."

"Good evening," Derrick backed a few steps away from the table then turned and left.

He left the club and headed towards the wharf. He was scheduled to meet Bryce at the Black Keg Pub.

He really didn't have a lot of information for Bryce, but at least he'd made the first move and his foot was in the door. Despite his optimistic swing on the conversation, Bryce was not very happy with him. Derrick knew that he needed to make this better – his life depended on it. The meeting was short which suited him. Although she enjoyed the money he brought in, he knew his wife would be worried.

Chapter Thirteen

Sky met Raven at the door and embraced her as if she was never letting go, "I've been so worried about you!"

"I'm fine Grandmother."

"You look so thin and tired. Have you been sleeping?"

"Not much. With Alex under my roof, the only time I had to search for Bryce has been late at night."

"Raven, did you take my diary."

"Yes, I am sorry, but I couldn't help it."

"Is that the real reason you're after Bryce?"

"Yes, but that isn't the only reason."

"Raven, this man is insane and very dangerous. He almost killed your grandfather and I."

"I know, but I have to do this; it's a matter of honor."

"But it isn't your place, dear."

"I am ready for this Grandmother."

"I thought I was, too."

"I don't want to fight with you. I've missed you so much!"

"Oh Raven, I've missed you too. Are you doing all right?" I know you and your father didn't always see eye – to – eye, but I also know that you loved him and your brother with all of your heart. I did too," Sky cried, embracing her grandchild again.

"I know Grandmother."

"Come along, your rooms are ready. Are you hungry?"

"Always!"

"Cook has all of your favorites prepared and the servants are waiting in the great hall." Raven had always been a favorite amongst the servants because she always treated them with kindness and respect. A soft smile crossed her face, *it's nice to be surrounded by people I love.* She hadn't realized how home sick she'd been, how alone she'd felt. Raven ate until she could hardly breathe. Her grandmother led her upstairs and wished her sweet dreams. Raven stood at her window for a bit, watching the late-night traffic in Mayfair. – all of the elegant carriages making their way to another party or perhaps on their way home. She felt disconnected from her surroundings which she laid at Alex's feet. He invaded her thoughts night and day. It made her angry that he thought more about a mysterious captain, whom he'd barely even glimpsed, instead of her. It made her crazy; especially because she and this mystery woman were one in the same! Her dream lover held her close and kissed her senseless.

She awoke with a start and, for a moment, didn't know where she was. It wasn't quite daylight yet, but she went ahead and poured water onto the basin and did her morning toilet. An hour or so later, her maid knocked lightly on the door, presenting her with a light breakfast. The maid informed Raven that her grandparents wanted her downstairs in an hour.

Chapter Fourteen

Alex awoke after another restless night of strange dreams. It was always the same – starting with the woman captain and ending with Raven. He should have gone into Lily's and relieved this obsession with Raven.

He washed and dressed, then went down to meet his family in the morning room. It had been several weeks since he'd seen his family. Everyone had gathered around the table, but immediately got up to welcome their youngest brother home. They had wanted to go to him in Ireland, but he'd insisted that they not. They had a pleasant meal – always a good time to catch up. Adam was the oldest brother, followed by James, and Rafe. There was Sarah, the only sister, Miles, and Alex brought up the rear. Sarah was already in her second season. She'd broken several hearts last year. Adam planned to marry at the end of the year – a celebration they all looked forward to.

The butler interrupted their family time to announce Josh's arrival. Alex wasn't naïve to the looks exchanged between Josh and Sarah – nor were the older brothers. Alex would have to have a talk with Josh.

"I will see you all at the funeral," Alex excused himself. They would all attend the funeral for Raven's father and brother later in the day. "I will be joining the duke's family at his request but I will see you after the services." He nodded to his brothers and sister as he and Josh left the room. As they made their way to the Admiralty Alex asked Josh, "Do you have designs on my sister?"

Josh balked at the question. In his mind he'd hidden his affections well.

"No, Alex, I know my place."

"What's that supposed to mean?"

"I'm a younger son with no future," Josh said bluntly.

"You are one of the best men I know, Josh. You captain you own ship, and you've fought bravely beside my brothers."

"Yes, but I have no property and no chance of inheriting."

"Sarah has a large dowry with a small estate in Hampshire."

"I would not offer for a woman I could not take care of on my own merit."

"I've never seen her look at any man the way she looks at you; and they all have everything you don't. So, I wouldn't just write this one off, my friend."

"Since when have you become such a relationship expert."

"I am not by any means, but I do think my near-death experience effected my opinion on a few things."

"Oh, so you are ready to admit you have feelings for Lady Raven?"

"Just what are you talking about?"

"Oh, it's okay for you to ask me personal questions…?

"That's right, I am still your commanding officer, at least for the next day or two."

"So you're really going through with it, huh?"

"Yes, it's time to join Robert in the shipping business. I can't imagine the other two in an office or on a ship." The two men walked a few more paces in silence before Alex spoke again, "Josh, I would support you and Sarah."

"I appreciate that, but…." The two men were suddenly interrupted by a man from the Admiral's office.

"The Admiral is ready to meet with you, sirs."

"Thank-you, Graves." As the men entered, they were surprised to see Blackthorn and Raven.

"Please, join us." The duke directed the young men towards some empty chairs across from he and Raven.

"Has something happened?" Alex asked, concerned.

"Yes, there has been a new attack." The Admiral stood and walked from behind his desk. "This time on British soil, a village just north of here. Several dead, women raped, and young men taken. The rest were locked in a church and, pardon my lady…."

"It's fine, sir. I have seen his work in Ireland. He attacked one of our smaller villages."

"It's sad business. We must put an end to it. Steele, be ready to sail with the morning tide."

"Aye, sir." Steele said with a salute.

"And you, Knight. Are you up to one last assignment?"

"Aye, sir."

"Very well, gentlemen, you have your orders." Raven and Alex's eyes met and he smiled and saluted as he and Josh left the office. Josh said he would send orders to the crew right away to ensure they were sober and ready to set sail in the morning.

"Thank you, Josh," Raven said as she followed the men outside. "May I have a moment?"

"Yes, of course, my lady. What's on your mind?"

"Alex, please be careful. This man, Bryce, is insane."

"I know, he won't catch me off-guard again, I promise. I will see you at the castle before the service, my lady."

Thank you, Alex." It felt strange to return to the formalities of polite conversation after having been so comfortable with one another over the last two weeks."

Chapter Fifteen

John Bryce sat in a tavern, waiting for Derrick. He hoped he was holding up his part of this deal. The man had no backbone at all, but he was motivated. Bryce had no qualms about threatening his family. After all, he already slept with Derrick's wife. For once, being a gentleman had it advantages. Albeit, not being one had many more, Bryce smirked. Derrick felt a cold shiver run down his spine as he noticed the look in Bryce's eyes; the man was Satan reincarnated. Bryce waved him over, "Sit down."

Back at Blackthorn castle, Sky spoke with Sherman, "Have you made the necessary changes?
"Yes, your grace, I have."
"Hopefully it won't be necessary. It should have been finished years ago. It would have saved so many lives."
"You couldn't have known, Sky," Sherman tried to reassure her.
Part of me knows that, but it still weighs heavy on my heart."
"I know, my girl."
Sky chuckled, "I haven't been a girl for some time now!"
"I still remember the first day you walked on board and told us that you were the captain," Sherman smiled, remembering, "You were so brassy and bold, but you made it work, girl."
"No, we made it work, my dear friend."

Blackthorn and Raven entered the study, "We're not interrupting, are we?" the duke shook Sherman's hand.

"No, dear, you know me. I've just got my nose in everyday matters as I always must."

"Hmm," the duke smiled, not fooled for a moment by his beguiling wife.

Raven excused herself, brushing their cheeks with a kiss.

"I'll be off to see to your business, ma'am," Sherman nodded his respect for the couple.

When he'd closed the door behind him the duke turned to his wife, "What is it you are up to, or… not up to?"

"There is a little something I must tell you, dear," the Sky admitted.

"Oh, like the fact that Raven is the captain that saved Knight?"

"Well, yes, as a matter of fact, exactly like that."

"But there's more?"

"I just can't allow her to do this by herself. And you, well, your health must be considered."

"I won't let you do this Sky."

With a little smile, "Yes, dear, you will."

"Alex, Josh, sail with the tide in the morning. Let them handle this, please," the duke implored.

"Do you think you can stop her?" she challenged.

"No, but you can."

"But I won't."

The duke snorted, "You think she has a better chance than two war heroes?"

"Yes, as a matter of fact, I do!" Both hands on her hips, she stared boldly at her husband.

"Sky, I can't, I won't allow this!"

"You can't stop it, darling."

"Raven is not you!"

"No, but she is more me than she is her father. Come, dear, I don't want to fight."

"I don't either, dearest," he took her lovingly in his arms, "but, I just can't lose any more of the people that I love, Sky. Can't you understand that?"

Raven stood just outside the door, listening to her grandparents. She knew she would have to leave right after the funeral. She sent a message to Michael directing him to prepare to sail. This was her destiny and she would not fail. And she certainly would not allow any more people she love get hurt. Not even Alex Knight. She realized, at that moment, just how much she loved him.

Chapter Sixteen

Alex arrived an hour later and was led into the family room. The mood was solemn but there was also another kind of tension in the air that he didn't quite understand. The duke called for the carriage and they filed out, each deep in their own thoughts. Alex was so proud of Raven. She held herself with all the grace and poise of a future duchess. It was still hard to thick of her that way; he remembers the days when she used to run as fast as she could to catch up to him and her brother. She was just a little tomboy that wanted to be a highway man or a pirate captain. A sudden shiver ran down Alex's spine; he quickly shook it off as the organ began to play. The somber service paid homage not only to the victims of a horrendous crime, but to the loved ones left behind to be tortured with the finality of the heinous act. As the family followed the caskets to the family crypt Alex stayed close to Raven. He noted she hadn't shed a single tear but he knew she loved her father and brother and expressed as much as they allowed. Both father and son were not ones to display emotion and discouraged it in those who loved them, especially from the women.

He'd noticed the absence of Raven's mother. Rumor had it she'd run off with her latest lover right after the murders. She knew she would never be a duchess, so she moved on to another fool. Raven had never been close to that woman; she knew how lucky she was to have her grandmother.

No one noticed the man lurking at the back of the procession. Bryce took a certain perverse pleasure out of watching the service – especially watching Sky. She should have been his. Of all his obsessions, this was his greatest – he derived great joy in watching her suffer. It was the one element that drove him all these years.

As they finished the final moments of the service, Raven walked beside Sky to place flowers on both tombs. She walked on Alex's arm to the duke's carriage. Next, they would have the banquet. Raven had always questioned the reason for this tradition. When the duchess explained to her that it was more for the living Raven finally understood. She, however, found greater comfort in Alex's nearness. Once they arrived back at the castle, they found Josh waiting for her grandfather and Alex. Blackthorn led them to his study. Raven, deciding she didn't like all the secrecy, made her way to the cubbyhole she'd hide in as a young girl, listening to her father and grandfather talk. She listened to their plans to sail at dawn and immediately set about putting her own plan into action. After the conversation she'd overheard between her grandparents, her grandmother asked her to leave the retribution to the men. Raven knew it would come as no surprise to her grandmother that she just couldn't do that.

When he learned Raven had retired for the evening, Alex couldn't hide his disappointment. It felt good to be there for her today and that, to him, was an unusual sensation.

"What's the problem," Josh asked.

"Nothing, it's been a long day," Alex mumbled. Josh knew better. He found it amusing that his longtime friend was falling in love. He wished he were able to act upon his own feelings of love, but that wasn't in the cards for him.

"Care to join me at the club?"

"I'll have to pass tonight, but I will see you at the ships. Have a good night Josh." As Alex let himself into his home he was surprised to see Sarah waiting for him. He smiled to himself. He knew she wasn't disappointed to see him, she was only disappointed that he was alone. She wished him goodnight and made her way upstairs. Alex grinned to himself and settled in for the evening. He should at least try to get some rest knowing full well dreams would invade his sleep.

Raven and Michael made their way silently to the cove where her ship was waiting. She felt her usual serge of excitement as she made her way aboard. As they readied to sail she went below to her cabin to change. She suddenly realized how alone she felt without her grandmother or Alex. She couldn't think about them now. She felt their lives were in danger and she just could not allow anything to happen to them.

Derrick and Bryce met at their normal spot. He told Bryce about what he stole from Admiral Gage's office. Bryce actually managed a smile, "So, they don't know who the female captain is?"

"Well done, Derrick. It's not often a man gets a second chance at life." Derrick cringed at the maniacal look in the other man's eyes and was glad his part in all of this was over. In John's mind, he knew the woman captain had to be Sky. No one else would have the courage to face his blade again. There could not be another woman that had her fire. He was about to achieve his life's dream. He would love to see Blackthorn's face when he found his wife missing on the morrow, but he knew he would have to be satisfied knowing he had finally won all. His crew looked uneasy at the sound of his hysterical laughter. They crossed themselves with the sign of the church.

Raven didn't waste a moment. They were headed for the last know sighting of Bryce. She could feel the tension on the wind and knew her life could end today. She had no other choice. She knew her grandmother was going to be angry; she could only pray she would understand what was driving her granddaughter.

Chapter Seventeen

Alex met up with Josh at four-thirty in the morning. They made their way to the ships in the dark, pre-dawn hours. Alex touched the still-tender spot on his side, he knew he had to be at his best, he suspected this would begin the most important fight of his young life. A brief, internal prayer strengthened his resolve.

Josh's thoughts followed a similar strain until he considered Sarah. He shook his head, he must stop thinking of her, she wasn't for him but, inexplicably, his thoughts never wandered far from her. He'd never experienced such an overwhelming force such as this.

The *Falcon* and the *Majestic* set sail just as the *Liberator* slid silently from the cove. Unbeknownst to Raven, Bryce, aboard the *Hawk*, lurked near the cove, not far off her starboard bow. Blinded by the rising sun, she hadn't spotted him yet. Bryce ordered his first mate to fire a warning shot over the bow of the ship. He could taste the victory at hand. Raven ordered all hands and prepared for battle. Bryce managed to catch her off guard. This didn't bode well for her. The ships fired several more rallies before the gun magazine on Raven's ship exploded. Men were in the water while others fought the blaze.

Bryce and his men boarded the limping ship and soon sounds of clanging steel, war cries and the screams of wounded men. Raven's crew fought valiantly, but the heavy battle fell to the attackers. Raven saw Michael fall and turned immediately to go to him. Bryce appeared out of nowhere and knocked her down. She lost hold on her sword and reached for the knife at her waist. He was too quick. His crazed laugh ended the battle as he twisted the captain's arms behind her back. He pulled the mask from her face and froze. He still did not have Sky. He knocked Raven unconscious and instructed his men to burn the ship. He dragged Raven's limp form to his own vessel and prepared to sail. The screams of Raven's crew, burning at sea, stirred her but for a moment before the blackness swept over her once more.

Alex and Josh saw the flames from twenty miles away. It took them over an hour to reach the grizzly sight. They immediately set their crews to salvaging the lives they could. One of the men they brought on board kept calling out for someone in Gaelic. *I know this man, why can't I place him?* Alex thought. Just then a gust of wind set ablaze the last remnant of a black sail. It was all that was left of his mysterious captain's ship. He rushed among the wounded sailors, asking who the culprit was that laid their ship to waste. Before long, a sailor confirmed his suspicion, the target of his search hijacked his captain.

Off the starboard bow came another ship; it was the duke's yacht. The duchess commanded the wheel. "Where is Raven?" she demanded. The Gaelic-speaking sailor called out, "The villain absconded with her ma'am." The color flooded from Sky's face at his words. The duke swung across to Alex's ship and took command.

"Sir, may I ask the purpose of your grave concern?"

"Bryce has Raven!"

Alex stepped back as if struck. *Bryce has the captain..., Raven..., one in the same. How can that be?* No wonder his dreams were as they were. He started at Josh's cry.

"A vessel approaching, starboard!" The lone passenger of the small dingy waved a white flag.

"I've a message for the duke and duchess of Blackthorn."

The duke lept to the railing, "You have my ear, man."

"If you want to see your granddaughter alive, you will follow instructions carefully."

"Sir, he cannot be trusted," Alex interjected.

"I know that commander, I have no choice," he turned back to the messenger, "What are your instructions?"

"You are to go the cove where it all began at six bells. Not one more than the two of you. If anyone else is present she dies. Do you understand?"

"Yes, we will be there. Alone." The second part directed at Alex.

Chapter Eighteen

"Gentlemen, No one must know her identity, I must have your word."

"Of course, your grace, but we mustn't let him get away with this."

"I know that cove better than anyone," the duchess spoke. "Are you gentlemen ready?"

"What do you have in mind, your grace?"

"Let's board my vessel; it's safe to talk in my cabin," she instructed. The men shot each other baffled looks but hastily followed the duke and duchess.

"Commander, I see you are trying to piece this mess together. Let me help. I am Sky O'Malley, former pirate captain and enemy of the East India Trading Company. A hefty reward for my capture remains today. Bryce once enjoyed the friendship of my husband and his first officer. The day I boarded their ship, I fell in love with the duke and he with me. Bryce became obsessed with me and plotted to have me to himself. One night he succeeded. He waylaid me on deck, dragged me to the hold, beat and raped me and left me for dead

"My love, you don't owe these men an explanation," the duke interrupted.

"Of course not, your grace," Alex agreed.

"But I do. I was determined to stay alive until my love could find me because I knew I was carrying our child. When the duke finally found me, I was more dead than alive.

Raven found my journals and she believes Bryce is her grandfather. She set out to avenge me and now he has her. I don't think he'll hurt her, it's me he wants. We have one small chance to rescue her without getting anyone else killed, but you must listen to me. There is one way through the narrow, shallow reef and no room for error.

The men listened to Sky and undoubtably knew what his grace saw in this lovely pirate captain. She was a woman that any man would die, and kill for, and Alex knew that Raven was his woman – cut from the same cloth. They set sail with each man and woman silent, intent on their mission.

The duke walked up behind Sky while she stood silently at the wheel. He captured her in his arms and kissed her tears. Together they thought about the many times they stood like this. He felt so much love for her, he wished she would stay behind but he knew that was nothing he could do or say to make that happen.

Alex gave his orders, went below deck to wash and poured himself a brandy. As he lay on his bunk he tried to sort out his feelings about Raven. He knew that if Bryce hurt her it would be the last time the villain ever laid hand on anyone. The man must be stopped. He prayed he had the strength, the will, the courage to stop him for good. Unsure when it happened, Alex knew Raven was the only woman for him. If she was anything like her grandmother he would be one of the luckiest man alive.

There was a knock at his door. He wasn't surprised to see Josh. Alex poured him a drink.

"What do you make of all this? And how are we supposed to explain this to the Admiral?

"I suspect he knows most of it. The duke and he have been friends since boyhood."

"Aye." They sat in silence and drank until they both fell asleep.

Chapter Nineteen

The duke lay quietly by Sky's side and watched her sleep. One of his favorite times, watching his love's peaceful rest. In the most trying of times she could lay it all down and sleep. He didn't believe he would ever know all of her secrets, but he expected she was one in a million. He knew his granddaughter inherited all that he admired in Sky.

"She has to be alright," the duchesses voice startled him.

"Of course she is, my love, you wouldn't have it any other way," he smiled and bent to kiss her soft, rich lips. She turned and held him close. His nearness gave her peace. Like mindedness brought them close, closeness gave them their strength for the day. They rose and dressed for battle.

Alex followed the map Sky made for him. They picked a small group of men trusted to guard Raven's secret identity and reputation. Alex did not concern himself with either. She was the woman he loved and he was determined to win her for himself. Years of running away from marriage disappeared overnight. So much depended on the mission's success. Alex and Josh stood ready to act at Blackthorn's signal. The tension thickened as the fog while they navigated the shallow channel.

The duke and duchess took the life boat to shore.

"Are you alright?" he asked his wife.

"I should have killed him when I had the chance," she replied with resolve.

Bryce waited on shore with several heavily armed men. He held his hand out to help Sky out of the boat. She slapped his hand out of the way. Instead of anger, he let out an eerie laugh. Chills ran down her spine.

"I want to see Raven. She is to get in the boat and head back to the *Regal*," she demanded.

"Your grace," Bryce mocked, "You are not in a position to give orders."

Sky bit her tongue to keep from saying what she really wanted to. The duke held her hand envisioning strength and support from his heart to hers.

"Go get the girl," Bryce turned and barked at the man standing nearest.

Sky steeled herself as the man dragged Raven along. Dried blood caked her hair and swelling twisted her features into a grotesque mask. Her torn clothes barely covered her bruised body.

In the nearby groves Josh grabbed Alex's arm. He felt the tension and heat of rage through Alex's coat and kept a steady hold on his friend.

Alex steadied his breathing and watched the duchess, herself still as a statue. The waiting drove him nearly mad. He nearly choked on his desire to mangle Bryce. And yet he waited. He, Josh, the men piled behind him, they waited.

Softly, Alex couldn't make out the words, Sky asked, "Are you alright dear? Raven?"

"Yes, grandmother. I wish you hadn't come. I would have escaped." At this statement Bryce hit

Raven hard across the face, knocking her to the ground. Josh tightened his hold on Alex as he felt him surge. The duke grasped his wife's hand, strengthening his resolve to kill the beast.

Raven rose determinedly to her feet.

That's my girl, Alex cheered inwardly, *you'll make an amazing duchess one day.*

Bryce raised his hand again but Sky grabbed it with all her force. "John, we've done all you asked. Let her go."

He looked at Blackthorn, "Take her and go. Sky stays with me."

"I'm not leaving my wife. If she stays, I stay."

Chapter Twenty

Alex wanted to follow Raven, but the lives of the
duke and duchess rested on his shoulders. Raven
would be safe for now. She climbed aboard the boat
and began rowing back to the yacht.

Bryce had the duchess bound and ordered her taken
to the *Hawk*. Alex's crew moved quietly through
the grove, toward the cove. He and Josh went
opposite ways once they reached the shore. The
duchess' accurate map and detailed planning
unfolded nicely.

As Bryce made his way back to his ship with the
duchess in tow a few of his men stayed behind to
tightly gag and bind the duke. They left him sitting
on the shore.

Moments later gunfire errupted from the direction
of the *Regal*. A silent form rushed from the grove's
cover to untie the duke. They ran toward the sound
of the shots. The enraged duke surged ahead of the
others. Alex commanded Josh to get the *Falcon* and
meet them at the yacht. He and the duke rowed the
life boat out to the *Regal*. They silently scaled the
rope ladder. As they reached the top Alex, behind
the duke, had to duck as a pirate's body, flung
overboard by the duke barely missed him. On top
they found mayhem on the yacht's deck. Alex
pressed through swinging swords and flying fists to
search for Raven. but there was no sign of her. The
duke approached a young crew member lying in
front of her cabin. He reached weakly towards the

duke, "Your grace, he has them, the women, sir."
The duke bent close as the young man's voice
faded. Alex watched as the crewman's body fell
limp. "What did he say, sir?"
"He said I am to go to the place where we played
together as kids. If I want to find the women alive, I
will come alone."
"Your grace, you know it's a trap."
"Of course, but what other choice do I have?"
Alex silently prayed for the lives of the two women
who'd been such an integral part of his life. "Sir, do
you trust this man at all?"
"At one time he was my best friend, aside from
Admiral Gage."
"May I ask what happened, sir?"
The duke thought pensively for a moment, "He
loathed that I had so much and he'd worked so hard
for the little he had."
"We'll get them back, sir. I swear it," Alex blood
stirred.
Josh joined them as the duke rose from the side of
the dead sailor, "Well, gentlemen, let's go get them
back." He turned to a crewman standing nearby,
"Allen, please see to the wounded and dead. I'll
want a full account when I return."
"Aye, sir," he gave a cursory salute and set about
his gruesome task.
The men moved to Josh's *Majestic* and made way
to his cabin. There the duke showed them the course
to a small island. "The good news, it's deserted; the
bad news, there's no cover for surprise.

They explored several different ways to approach the island finally deciding that Alex and Josh would swim in, each landing on opposite sides of the island. The duke and one sailor would row ashore. Hopefully it would create enough of a distraction for Josh and Alex to get ashore. Precise timing was crucial. Several groups of seamen would wait just offshore for the signal all was clear.

Chapter Twenty-One

Alex reached the shore first. He proceeded toward a clearing where he saw the Bryce with the duchess out in the open. He frantically looked for Raven and finally spotted her lashed to a tree, fresh blood stained the remnants of her shirt and her face freshly bruised. Alex swore under his breath that Bryce would live only long enough to regret the harm he'd inflicted. He checked his pistols and blade again; everything was ready so he settled in to wait quietly for the signal to move in.

On his way in, Josh found and disabled three guards. He settled behind some shrub to assess the scene. He saw Bryce and the duchess watching the shoreline where the duke disembarked from the boat and sent the sailor away. Several men moved forward to claim Blackthorn's weapons.

Bryce approached using Sky, hands tied at her back, as a shield. He stopped several feet away from the duke.

The duke and Sky silently gauged one another, their eyes locked.

"This meeting has come too late in our lives, Andrew," Bryce broke the silence. "I want to see your eyes as you realized I have destroyed you completely – taken everything that should be mine."

"Why should it all have been yours, John?"

"You honestly still don't know," Bryce's maniacal laughter filled the island. Chills swept even the most hardened of his men.

Alex remained focused on Raven. Josh was to free her while he assisted the duke in seizing Bryce and securing the duchess. The rest of the crew listened intently for their signal to row in and assist.

"I was the first born, Andrew, John confessed. "I am your bastard brother. That is why I attended the best of schools, along with you and Gage. It was all my father could or would do for me. The deaths of Charles and Tobias didn't sadden me at all. In fact, I was giddy with joy at their demise. I was that much closer to obtaining all that is rightfully mine. Yes, once you are dead, I will be the remaining heir and the dukedom mine.'

The duke wrestled in his mind how he'd missed it all these years. How could he have known. His father certainly offered nothing of having a bastard son. He shook the shock away, "Let Sky and Raven go. I'll abdicate the dukedom and it will be yours."

Bryce's crazed laugh assaulted the air again, "Oh no Andrew, that is not enough. You will be totally devastated once I finish with you."

"John, if you have any love or decency in your heart, you will let them go."

"I don't," Bryce smirked, "I want you to watch as I take your woman and granddaughter. When I am done, I will make Sky my duchess."

"John, do you really believe you can get away with this?"

Bryce shrugged, "Oh, I already have, brother dear." The smug look on his face turned to shock as he heard a large explosion. Another ship had entered the channel. The Admiral's warship bore down upon the island. Her crew clamored to set anchor and lower the gunboats.

Alex and Josh signaled and moved in with their men. As several boats made their way towards shore another loud explosion shook the air followed by several more. Flames engulfed the *Majestic*.

Bryce shoved Sky aside and focused his attack on Blackthorn. Alex reached the duchess' side. He cut her hands loose and helped her to her feet.

Josh freed Raven. She snatched the saber from the pirate Josh had impaled on his way to her. The two rushed over to assist in the capture of Bryce. Alex turned his attention from the battle, relieved to see Raven on her feet. He turned, blade searching for Bryce, but the intended target swung his sword wildly and slashed Alex's side. Alex staggered, blood rushed from the wound but he regained his feet to join the duke and Raven in pursuit of Bryce.

Raven reached him first but grew dizzy from exhaustion in her weakened state. Bryce laughed hysterically as he watched her strength fading. He moved to finish her when Alex lunged at him. Bryce dodged Alex's blow and stepped back. He was absolutely giddy surveying the deteriorating state of his adversaries.

The duke moved in to assist the failing warriors but Sky screamed at him to stop, "This is my fight," she commanded, "I'll finish what I should have forty years ago. I can do this my love." The duke stepped back, helped Raven to her feet and out of the fray.

He turned back to where steel clashed against steel.

Raven struggled to Alex's side.

Chapter Twenty-Two

Admiral Gage and his men hastened toward the fight.

"Back!" Sky yelled.

The men stopped short of the fight, aghast at their diminished role.

The battling duo matched blow for blow. As the skirmishes around them ended the bodies of Bryce's seamen littered the ground, only a few hung tenaciously to life. A circle formed around the pair. Raven left Alex's side to assist her grandmother if needed. But Sky held her own. One of Bryce's men, hidden in the grove, stepped out to join in the fray. Sky mocked, "What, John, you have to cheat to best a woman?"

Bryce turned but for an instant. Just long enough for Sky to plunge her sword deep in his chest. He turned, clutched at his heart, eyes wide. Sky's blade severed fingers as she ripped it from his chest. Blood pumped, unchecked, from the wound. He opened his mouth as if to speak but slumped to the ground without uttering a word.

Sky found herself in the duke's arms. She fell limp. The duke gently crouched, sat and cradled her securely in his arms.

Raven stood unmoved, unable to fathom the battle won. She regained her senses and turned to Alex. She nearly fell beside him and began tearing the tatters of her shirt to stanch the blood oozing from his wounds. Tears slid down her cheeks. Alex reached up with his good arm to tenderly wipe them away. "Raven," he looked deeply into her wearied eyes, "Will you be my wife? I can only love you more with each passing day." He pulled her down gently and held her close.

He sensed a shadow standing over them, he squinted in the sun.

"It took you long enough," Josh looked around, "Although not quite the romantic setting the woman might expect."

"And you are going to ask my sister…when?"

"We've had this discussion before. I'm not good enough for her, Alex. She deserves the best."

Admiral Gage overheard this and smiled to himself. Both men would be decorated for bravery, going above and beyond, *Sarah would be hard pressed to find a finer man.*

He stepped over to the duke and duchess. "My men are coming to get you out of here. We'll see that the wounded are aided and the dead, a proper burial at sea."

Raven lay in the comfortable stateroom. She struggled for consciousness. She'd been so shocked at Alex's proposal she'd not answered him. *In time* she thought as she succumbed to sleep.

Chapter Twenty-Three

Alex made his way to Raven's cabin. He was poised
to knock when a hand clasped his back. He turned,
expecting to see the duke, but the duchess cautioned
him instead, "Let her rest tonight."

"But she didn't answer my question."

"I know it is hard for a man who commands to
acccpt but she has waited for you her whole life."

"Yes, your grace."

"Call me Sky. It's what family does."

Alex turned and walked away, his step a little
lighter, *It's what family does.* He like that sound of
that.

They docked in London early the next morning.
Josh and Alex left with the Admiral to file reports.
The duke accompanied them. When they had a
moment alone, the duke clasped Alex's shoulder in
a strong squeeze, "If you ever hurt Raven, it's me
you'll have to answer to."

"Sir, I could never hurt her."

"See to it you don't."

Alex stayed away from Blackthorn castle for the
next few days. He spent time with his family, filling
them in on the details of his latest adventure. He
saved the proposal for last. He had, after all, not had
affirmation from Raven yet. When he spoke of it
aloud it seemed so foreign on the one hand, and so
natural on the other. He felt as if this relationship
with Raven had been the norm for years yet
scarcely a month had passed since he'd been

annoyed with her presence following mysterious pirate's intervention to save his life.

His brothers slapped him on the back, shook his hand and congratulated him over and over with much laughter and joviality. Sarah hugged him tightly, brushed his cheek with a kiss, "I am so happy for you dear brother. Raven is getting a fine man." While her wishes were sincere, he knew the source of the sadness in her eyes. He would have to have another talk with Josh. *I think she'd live in the gutters if it meant being with him.* He and Josh both received promotions upon their return. Between his new post and her inheritance, they could live quite comfortably.

Alex would miss the Admiralty but he felt confident his new opportunities would be lucrative and he would not be sailing off, leaving Raven behind. He smiled, he felt certain life would be anything but dull with Raven.

Raven slept for a full day. She was a little shaken that Alex hadn't come by to see her. Her grandmother told her they would attend a small dinner party at the Grayson's. The last thing she wanted was to go back to town, but Sky would have none of it.

Alex left a meeting with the duke after securing his approval for a small, quiet wedding. He'd gotten the license from the Bishop. He couldn't wait for the evening. He had one more errand to run; this one he wasn't so much looking forward to. He was on his way to tell Lily he would no longer be her protector. He made his way through the exclusive community and took the stairs to the porch two steps at a time. He didn't see the duke's carriage.

Raven was just about to call out to him when a beautiful young woman opened the door and threw herself into Alex's arms. That was all Raven needed to see. She pressed the driver to return her to the castle immediately. If only she'd stayed a few moments longer she would have seen Alex leave a very angry woman on the steps.

Alex hurried to dress for the dinner party. He planned to ask Raven for her hand again that evening, this time with the duke and duchess' blessing. He felt so happy and so confident they would share in a splendid life.

Raven arrived home with unshed tears brimming in her eyes. So far, she'd not run into anyone. As she opened the door she was surprised to see her grandmother waiting for her. Sky saw the tears as they fell to Raven's cheeks.

"What happened, child?" she brushed Raven's hair from her face.

Raven couldn't bring herself to say out loud what she'd seen. Sky held her until the tears stopped. Sniffling, Raven told her grandmother what she'd seen, "It hurts so much."

"Raven, dear, you know men in Alex's position keep mistresses. It's a very old, and accepted practice.

"Did grandfather keep one?"

"Yes, he did."

"And you were okay with that?"

"Not by any stretch of the imagination. I wanted to run her through with my blade."

"Well, did you?"

"No, in time it all worked out. Give Alex a chance dear. Let him explain to you what you saw today."

"I don't know if I can."

"You must. I love you Raven, dear. Lie down now and get a bit of rest."

Raven hugged her neck, "I love you so, grandmother."

Chapter Twenty-Four

Alex took extra care in his appearance for the evening. He scoffed at his trembling hands. A hardened veteran should not be afraid of asking someone to marry him. But Raven wasn't just anyone. She was the bravest, strongest and most beautiful woman he'd ever known. He took a deep breath, looked himself in the mirror and gave a slight nod.

His valet stepped in and told him his brother requested his presence. He was shocked to find the duchess waiting for him. She told him Raven had seen him with his mistress.

"Your grace," he swore, "I was there to end our relationship. She means nothing to me. Raven is my all."

"I am not the one you need to convince, young man."

"Thank you, your grace."

"Good luck, son."

Sky arrived back at the castle to find Raven still in her dressing gown, "I'm not going, grandmother. I don't want to see him."

"Yes, dear, you are. I've just spoken to Alex. Raven, you need to give him a chance."

"You went to see Alex?" Raven turned on her grandmother. Oh, for sure I'll never be able to face him now," she threw herself on her bed.

Sky sat beside her granddaughter and smoothed her hair, "Yes, Raven, you will. And it will be the beginning of a strong marriage. I don't want you to miss out on the wonderful love I know the two of you will share. You must give him a chance. Now, get up and dress."

Alex and his family arrived promptly at eight. He scanned the room searching for Raven but he couldn't find her. His heart pounded in his chest, so afraid she wouldn't give him a chance to speak to her again.

The duke and duchess entered the foyer. Alex heard the murmurs and fixed his eyes on the door. Raven followed her grandparents. She looked stunning, he had never seen a more beautiful woman. He knew he could never love anyone else as much as he loved her at this moment. He had to make her listen, he simply would not accept a life without her.

Raven looked about the room as she followed her grandparents. When her eyes met his she dropped them immediately. When she looked up again, she looked everywhere but where he was standing. She moved in the opposite direction, speaking to those who greeted her, she smiled, albeit half-heartedly, and exchanged pleasantries with her family's friends. Her heart was not in this. She looked as though she wanted to be anywhere but where she was.

At the dinner table, Alex tried to meet her eyes but she talked to his brother and sister, without so much as a glance his way. After dinner, the men retired to the study for brandy and cigars. Alex situated himself near the duke, "Sir, do you think I have a chance with her tonight."

Blackthorn looked about the room as he spoke, "I'm not sure, but you need to get this settled or she will dig her heels in."

"Yes sir. Thank you."

"Good luck son, I think you are going to need it. Should you be successful keep this in mind, if, in the event the future offers, shall we say, indiscretions, the outcome can only be worse." The corners of his mouth turned up and his eyes twinkled at the thought of his granddaughter's wrath should this ever come up again.

The men joined the ladies in the music room. Raven sat quietly by the duchess. She wouldn't meet his eyes. The only thing that came to mind for Alex was to carry her out, give her no more opportunity to ignore him. He ordered his coach to bring his carriage around. He hastily scribbled note to his family and the duke. If she wouldn't come to him, he would kidnap her.

He walked to the front of the room, smiled and nodded to the duchess. He walked boldly up to Raven, lifted her off of her feet and carried her across the room and through the front door.

The duke started after him but Sky placed her hand on his arm and smiled. The butler handed him the note from Alex. He looked at Alex's brothers who'd just received their note. The lot of them burst out laughing and lifted their glasses.

"We should take ourselves to my home so that we may be there when they decide to return."

"Grand idea, old man," Miles hailed.

Adam broke in, "Your grace, I do apologize for my younger brother's action. I will be your second if you would like to address him concerning the matter."

Blackthorn smiled, "Thank you Adam, let's hope that isn't necessary.

Raven beat on Alex's back, "Put me down! You've totally ruined me and shamed my family."

Alex put her on her feet, "You gave me no other choice, Raven." He closed her mouth with a kiss. After the briefest of moments, she pushed him back with all of her might, "You, I saw you with that woman. I saw her grab you!" Raven struggled to free herself from his arms.

"I haven't been with another since a pirate captain saved my life." He felt her soften, still in his hold, but facing away. "I repeatedly confused the two of you until I discovered the truth. I swear, Raven, I will spend the rest of my life making it up to you. Please, I beseech you, make me whole, become my wife." She turned in his arms and stared boldly into his eyes, "It would be my honor, sir, to become your wife." He gave her a soft kiss and helped her onto the carriage. Several hours later he directed his driver to Blackthorn castle. They'd been alone for several hours, so they must wed soon. Alex was fine with that. He couldn't make her his, and his alone soon enough. For someone who shunned commitment he anxiously awaited the moment she would become his wife.

Chapter Twenty-Five

The Bishop of Calvary officiated at the wedding of the decade. As Josh helped him with his cravat Alex confessed "I don't believe I've ever been so nervous."

"It's a big moment, my friend. I wish you all the best."

"Thank you, Josh., I'll return the favor when you finally ask for my sister's hand in marriage."

"You know where I stand on that."

"I won't let it rest. I am determined you will have a change of heart," Alex smiled as they left for the cathedral.

The young men stood at the alter as the organ started playing. The duchess waited quietly, for her husband to join her.

Raven walked slowly beside her grandfather. As they came down the aisle she looked left and right, smiling, astonished at all those who'd come to witness the most important day of her life. Once her eyes met Alex's, however, he held her there. She glanced away only briefly as the duke brushed her cheeks with kisses and held her hand just one more moment before he let her go.

The moment their eyes locked, Alex stopped breathing. As she floated down the aisle towards him in an elegant gown of lace and pearls he envisioned soft, wispy clouds. If he dared breathe she would float away. But as soon as she left the duke's gentle hold, she reached for his hand with the gentlest touch. The Bishop smiled at the loving pair. The world continued in slow motion until he spoke the words husband and wife. Alex paused as he savored the moment Raven became his wife and he kissed her gently, with the greatest respect. He drew his face away from hers and looked into her loving eyes. As a huge smile cracked his face, Raven reached up to brush her smile against his.

The Admiral's palace held the reception where guests mingled and visited with the new couple. Raven and Alex escaped after an hour for a respite on the terrace. "Alex, I've never asked how you felt about my becoming the Duchess of Blackthorn one day."

"It won't change my love for you," he smiled and kissed her forehead.

They turned when they heard a voice coming from across the terrace.

"You shouldn't be out here alone," Josh admonished Sarah as she walked up beside him.

"I'm not alone," she smiled.

"Sarah, we can't do this. You know where I stand." She held his eyes for a moment before she reached up and kissed him. "I am tired of that excuse," she said resolutely as she stepped back.

Alex looked back at his new bride and smiled, "I believe there is another wedding in the very near future."

The End